A GEM OF A

Andrew Noble

For Vivian
με αγάπη
και Φιλακία

Feb '24

ARTHUR H. STOCKWELL LTD.
Torrs Park   Ilfracombe   Devon
Established 1898
www.ahstockwell.co.uk

British Library Cataloguing-in-Publication Data.
A catalogue record for this book is available
from the British Library.

All the characters in this book have no existence outside the
imagination of the author, and have no relation whatsoever to anyone
bearing the same name or names. They are not even distantly inspired
by any individual known or unknown to the author, and all incidents
are pure invention.

ISBN 978-0-7223-3796-7
Printed in Great Britain by
Arthur H. Stockwell Ltd.
Torrs Park   Ilfracombe
Devon

Acknowledgements

In the greater scheme of things, despite my brain and fingers working long hours to complete this book within something approaching a reasonable time frame, there are some people whom I should like to offer my thanks and appreciation for their kind help and support:

My thanks go to my colleagues at work, for their encouragement, particularly Danny, Israela, Alisa and Gordon. Others, who know their role, shall always be remembered for their kindness. For some invaluable input and an insight into a world I would otherwise never have been able to get such a good look at, my thanks go to Jet Black, Steve, Kevin, Tristan and the other performers whom I have met on the cabaret and hen-night circuit. Such experiences and conversations were, and shall always be, priceless! For Jonathan, who knows me so well, and who has stayed the best of friends for so long, my simple thanks for his ability to put my wild ideas into some sort of rational order. To Declann, who remains a firm friend after all that I have put him through, I thank him for his help and advice. Nick, who has been a great help and webmaster, I thank in the solid knowledge that without him no such web design would ever have seen daylight. To my family, my appreciation goes for their support and bearing. It is not easy to remain in a constant state of 'knowing what he is going on about', yet they have borne this mantle with dedication, if not always with total understanding. My love for them remains unconditional. My thanks and love to the Irish contingent of friends that I am lucky to have, for the time they took to listen to, consider and read through my ideas and chapters during the infancy period of this book. For some sage advice, I wish to thank Gordon Hausmann most sincerely.

A writer of far more fame than I could hope to attain at this time, once said that everyone has a book inside them. My thanks to my publishers for their faith in me, and making this all become a reality. The ability to be a good storyteller helps, but primarily it is the realisation that the book inside you dictates when you shall sit down and write it, rather than you sitting down and trying to force it out. It has for a long time been this book's aim to reach the outside world beyond the confines of my brain, so I wish it happiness and wellbeing, as I do to all of you who read it.

The Author

Andrew Noble was born in Bournemouth and grew up in the area, attending the Arnewood School in New Milton.

Following the successful attainment of a diploma in travel and tourism, he joined the travel industry, working locally as a travel agent with two travel agencies, before moving to London, where he worked for SABENA Belgian Airlines.

A period of five years in South Africa has left him with the best of friends around him, and the best perspective with which to appreciate life and all that it throws at us. It was in South Africa that Andrew joined Singapore Airlines and discovered in more detail what a wonderful place the Far East, and in particular Singapore, can be.

Having travelled the world since the age of seventeen, Andrew feels that travel, and particularly travel to places beyond the tourist belt, is the best education in life that one can find.

He returned to London eleven years ago, and lives and works there, still in the airline industry. As frequently as possible, visits to South Africa help to retain his sanity on an even keel, though London itself has a lot to offer and continues to inspire Andrew for future works.

Visit Andrew Noble at: www.andrewnoble.net

Contents

Chapter One

Coming Home

It could be argued about, and agreed upon, that for him to try to do all the Christmas shopping in one day, just one week before the start of the holidays, was questionable in terms of sanity and tolerance. Had he overheard you saying what lunatic would ever think of negotiating Orchard Road at such a busy time of year, he would have raised his eyebrows ever so slightly, and mentioned something about the heat, the sun, and their effects on Englishmen, not only now, but at any time of the year.

The fact was that after working tirelessly to secure contracts for export, the arduous and much delayed task of bookkeeping, and a long weekend of playing host to prospective investors, Hector found the scrum and surge of the many shops and stores along Orchard Road a blessing in disguise, as it took his mind off more pressing problems. Dodging tourists who were frozen to the spot outside the Mandarin Hotel gazing in awe at orchids and concrete, two things in which Singapore excelled, Hector swept into C. K. Tang's, and aimed purposefully for their Christmas department. Although well known for their range of stock, variety of choice, and old-fashioned Oriental know-how, C. K. Tang's managed to stage a remarkable Christmas department. Upon entering, you were enveloped instantly in the sugary warmth of a cold night by the fire toasting crumpets or marshmallows, and in no way whatsoever reminded you that you were standing on the bustling island republic, which by now had become such an important trading post and crossroads of Asia, admired by many, feared by some, and repeatedly visited by a few.

Rumour had it that if Christ the Redeemer was to make his second coming to this earth, he would have to change planes at Changi, the location of Singapore's notorious prison/Second World War POW camp and, nowadays, just as well known for its self-styled Airtropolis. The thought of travelling through Changi later that day made Hector's stomach turn over. He wasn't as fast a mover as he had once been, even though at times he kidded himself otherwise, and pushed full throttle on all engines in order to whip some young pup in the sports facilities enjoyed by his employees at the plant. After all, it was good karma for the boss himself to mix and mingle with his workforce and, for the majority of the time, everyone loved having Mr Barnes join in. No matter how hard people tried to relax, though, and share jokes or food, it seemed that with the boss around (or rather quietly sitting in the corner pretending to read the *Straits Times* when in fact you knew he could see all and hear all) no one felt totally at ease. The boss wasn't a tyrant (he had made sure everyone received the Christmas bonuses, drinks and token gifts), it was just that you knew he wanted, or rather insisted on knowing absolutely everything about his workers, team leaders and sales force.

Hector emerged from C. K. Tang's after a short but easier than first expected sojourn around the Christmas department and clothing floors. Upon leaving the huge main entrance, he felt as though he were swimming against a strong human tide of Australian pensioners who were in transit for a day or two. Relief visited the wrinkles creased across Hector's forehead as he sighted Alex, his driver, who had stopped the car near to Tang's, thereby providing Hector with a fast getaway from the thronging and sweat-drenched crowds.

"Find the easiest way back to the office for me, Alex," Hector grumbled as he swung his tall frame into the soft leather interior of the car.

Alex said nothing. Having closed the door for Hector, Alex strode back round to the driver's door, pulled on his white gloves, flexed his fingers as if he were a gynaecologist about to delve where no one had delved before, and swiftly, but professionally, manoeuvred the car out into the main flow of Orchard Road. After a cooling, air-conditioned journey of no more than ten minutes, the car arrived outside Hector's office and parked under a large sign than announced in grand tones, 'The Barnes Oriental Gem Emporium' in gold lettering on a glossy navy-blue background.

"Wait for me here, please," said Hector to Alex as he got out of the car. "My suitcase is with Jean, and can be put in the car to go directly to the airport. I shouldn't be more than a quarter of an hour."

Alex nodded in acknowledgement, and, noticing a smear on the driver's door of the car, gave it some immediate attention with one of his gloves, which pleased Hector. He had always liked Alex, not only for his vast and skilled knowledge of Singapore's streets and alleys, but also his deftness, loyalty and pride in one's work. These were qualities that seemed rarely observed these days, and they always struck a chord with Hector, as they tended to make members of staff stand out amongst others.

Such a description equally applied to Jean. Rather than calling herself a secretary or PA, which seemed to suit other office girls, Jean would always introduce herself as Mr Barnes' Assistant, the capital A being entirely intentional. Already a devoted employee for more than twenty years, Jean shared, observed and, from time to time, improved by suggestion the running of Hector's business.

Jean Cutting had travelled around the Far East for most of her life, the boarding-schooled daughter of a military couple who had originated from Littlehampton, though they had always preferred to keep that particular detail to themselves.

Jean, who by now was into her early fifties, had married young, soon discovered how awful men can be once they think that they own you, and had run out of a forces' New Year's Eve dance in Rangoon. Not being inclined to look back after deciding to run forward, she had settled a neat but comfortable divorce, since scandal can spread so quickly in ex-pat territories. The fruit from these events was a pleasant home and the reliance on an old-fashioned, but well-preserved, compact and foam puff, for even when you are used to these climates, there's nothing more soothing than taking the time to regularly powder one's nose in the pure sense of the expression.

Perhaps on purpose, to somehow suppress her love of sparkling jewels, and the creations made by the big designers whom Hector Barnes had supplied for so many years, Jean didn't wear much jewellery herself. What little she owned, however, was of the highest quality in an understated but chic manner, which was rather like Jean herself.

It was whilst she was biting her bottom lip, and trying to secure the clasp to a slim but well-made bracelet, that Hector appeared from a lift, marched past her, and started to shuffle papers on the large desk in his office. Jean hovered.

"Is there still no word from Thomas? It really is too rude of him," muttered Hector under cover of a white linen handkerchief he was making the most of. "After all, it's not as if I'm taking the midday train up to town from Brighton to visit my brother for the weekend, is it?"

"No, not at all," clipped Jean, who having averted her eyes from Hector's mid-face conjuring trick, which revealed a shiny nose and no sign at all of a small dove, focused herself on the matter in hand. "Your plane lands at Heathrow at around six in the morning, local time, so if there is any further advice via phone or email, I will be sure to let you know." Jean straightened the shuffled papers as if she had just completed reading the evening news, and as Hector inserted several envelopes into various pockets around his hand luggage, she gently tendered a pen for him to make a few final strokes of his signature on contracts that would take form in his absence.

It had been longer than he cared to think of since he had completely relaxed on a holiday without any strings attached, business lunches and dinners, or even the dreaded karaoke club circuit which his Japanese clients loved so much. Now, finally, knowing that he could leave Jean to guide his ship, and Alex to see all, hear all, and say nothing, he actually felt a pang of tense excitement. England for Christmas and New Year, and, after the family tied duties of meeting a brother, whom he had neither seen nor heard from since a brief appearance at a family wedding some eighteen months before, he had decided to go to Ireland for a few days. Many friends and associates had reminded Hector that, at this time of year, it was not somewhere you unpacked a bikini. He had smothered a giggle at the notion, and moreover the mental image of trying to climb into a bikini on an Irish beach in mid-January. Nevertheless, it remained a country full of happy memories, and, without an abundance of various gems to be mined, cut, polished and sold, he was confident of the 'complete getaway factor', which Jean had so often reminded him of the necessity of having.

By now, Alex had discreetly removed the solid and well-made suitcase, and, with Jean holding the lift door open, he had returned to the car and loaded the heavy case into the boot.

Hector passed Jean the freshly signed papers, and, with an ever so slight hesitance in touch, they embraced clumsily and wished each other a merry Christmas, happy New Year, and bon voyage all rolled into one with a snort of laughter and garnished with smiles.

"Don't worry about Thomas, he'll appear once he knows you're around on his turf," Jean said softly as she escorted Hector to the car. "Make sure you have some time to yourself, catch up with old friends, eat and drink the best of everything, and return safe but rested. We have a lot of ideas to float next year, after all, so we'll need you back with your battery fully recharged."

Hector paused with his hand on the car door as Alex took his place in command of the car, and looked intently into Jean's recently powdered face. "All that you have just said to me applies to you too. I can't run this place without you behind me, so make the most of my not barking around the place for a while. Go and visit your cousin in Wellington, or the godchildren in Melbourne, but, for God's sake, go somewhere. Don't stay here over the holidays this time. We've done that all too often, so for once, Jean, my dear, take a pinch of your own advice." With that said, his eyes twinkled slightly.

With Jean closing the car door and mouthing something through the window to him, Alex decided that enough was enough, that the plane to London wouldn't wait, not even for Hector Barnes, and the car sailed off into the evening traffic and snaked its way through the busy streets until he could take a few short cuts, follow the beach road, and, before long, deposit Hector in front of a carpeted and florally decorated check-in desk.

Jean had prearranged everything, of course, so, in what seemed like no time at all, Hector was seated on the aircraft and departing on time from Changi. For a moment he wondered what it was that he had been so anxious about, as he realised that, with Jean to see to all his plans, there never would be any problems.

The 747 powered itself gracefully into the night sky over the straits of Malacca, amazing the couple from York who were seated at the rear of the plane wondering how such a big and heavy beast of a thing could get so high in the sky in such a short time, what time was it in Perth, and had Maggie fetched the kids from the pool yet.

Some twelve hours later, the aircraft emerged from beneath the clouds and effortlessly curtsied onto the runway at Heathrow on a dark and frosty morning. After a long but generally uneventful flight, during which Hector had cuddled several tumblers of good malt whisky, and been entertained by a rotund Russian businessman trying to get the in-flight movie system working on his seat, the first glimpse of London from the sky was that of gross overcrowding, an excess of electricity, and, for such an early hour, the hectic amount of movement on the streets.

Having claimed his luggage and negotiated the various channels and queues, which make up the rabbit warren of a modern-day airport terminal, he took a taxi into central London and registered at the Winchester Hotel, which, thanks to Jean, had been pre-booked to accommodate his early arrival.

With still no contact made or message received from Thomas, he showered and took a few hours' sleep after his long journey. At some point in the dying hours of daylight, he arose from his adequate bed in the stereotypical de luxe chain-hotel room and went for a walk. He had forgotten how short winter days were in England, as most of his previous visits to London had been in spring or summer months, and the climate change from Singapore ensured that he was enveloped snugly in his navy-blue full-length woollen overcoat, with the collar turned up to prevent the icy wind from licking the back of his neck.

After a stroll down memory lane, visiting several small streets in Mayfair that were filled with memories of his youth, then traversing St James's Park and being delighted in finding his old tobacconist still in business, despite the current trend for not smoking, he retired to a small pub on the corner of Jermyn Street. He sat with a plate of sausage and cheese, enjoying a glass of Guinness. Such are the small pleasures of someone who has made his home far away, and yet revels in nostalgia stimulated by the senses.

At this point, his senses were in overdrive as he tingled with the pleasure of not only what was being consumed, but also the warm glow and atmosphere of the pub. There were small groups of office workers who had met after work for the famous, but totally fictional, 'just one drink', and who would be on the receiving end of some sobering judgement from their spouses when they would finally fall through their suburban front doors some hours later. There was a group of girls from the department store round the corner, kicking off a night out and staying farewell to a colleague. Huddled together around a small table, and playing imaginary chess with tonic bottles and shot glasses, their topic was hinged on which den of sinful pleasures to visit first in Soho once they had downed a couple of drinks 'just to keep the cold out'.

Squashed in between all the chattering and cackling was a man of somewhat weathered appearance. Hector studied the man discreetly. Plump, and yet well padded by a thick woollen jumper, with a beard in need of some attention, and fat fingers, under which lay some premium London grime, the man was reading an evening paper, only pausing periodically to take a swig from his ale. Though Hector had seen the man outside earlier, selling newspapers, it made a nice picture now to see him, warmed by the pub, quenched by the ale, and reading the paper as if he were the editor himself passing sentence on the final edition before going to press.

As most of the pub's customers were finishing work for the Christmas holidays, the overall mood was jovial, and you could not fail to notice the trouble that the landlord had gone to with all the decorations that wound their way from ceiling to floor, and chains of tinsel which were draped from one corner of the window to the other. Dangling from the light by the door, with the air of an assassin, was a twig of mistletoe which the crowd of girls had now set their eyes on, and were beginning to encircle in anticipation that one of the young men from the other crowd would sooner or later surrender to their spell, and throw himself into their clutches for a touch of festive charm.

Hector had enjoyed the food and drink, but, except for the newsvendor, who had been at lengths to preserve his privacy in such a busy little bar, as indeed Hector had been himself, there seemed to be a lack of self-control in the air, the fault of which could not be laid at the feet of Christmas cheer. As much as Hector had seen in Singapore, young people there certainly knew how to conduct themselves, and the colourful language being bandied about the pub would have been quite alien to the Singaporean ear. He wasn't against the young ones having a good time, but their tongues would surely be their undoing at some point in the future. On this point he had to admit to himself with a sigh as he crossed Piccadilly that London was not the place it used to be.

The following morning, feeling much more in step with the time zone, Hector checked for messages from Jean with the concierge. He settled his bill and took a taxi to Waterloo, from where he went by train to Dorset, preparing himself for a Christmas with friends who had known him since he had been a young man keen to get into the jewellery business and, following a tip-off from a helpful acquaintance in the industry, had first travelled east in search of his fortune.

It had made perfectly good sense to get the train out of London when he did, for Hector knew that, had he remained another day in the capital, the crush and stampede to get away by any means of transport would have been unbearable.

The journey lasted just over two hours, and, in between glancing out of the window at the wintry and frost-pinched countryside, he did a crossword in one of the daily papers, and thumbed through the in-flight magazine, which he had taken from the aircraft upon arrival at Heathrow. Amid all the adverts for luxury scarves, make-up that claimed to be a saviour in the battle against wrinkles and crow's feet, and tempting adverts for classic brands of various spirits and liqueurs, Hector spotted the jewellery. His eyes settled on a fantastic creation from one of the large Italian makers, famed, as the advert pointed out, for their elegance and finesse.

"A nice piece, that is. Bit over the top for Christmas, though, isn't it?"

Hector turned to find a young man staring into his eyes. "It is of the optimum quality and best craftsmanship," replied Hector. "That is why the price is what it is. Think of it as an investment."

The young man's mouth curled slightly into a half-smile. "The piece I was referring to is the one what is wearing the thing. Now that would be worth a bit of investing!" said the man with a light chuckle, a hint of lechery veiled behind it. "How much is it anyway?" asked the young man, and, when Hector pointed to the price which was written in small characters in the corner of the page, the young man sat with his mouth open for a good thirty seconds.

"Close that, will you? there's a terrible draft coming across," smiled Hector, and having made the minimum of introductions, from which he learnt that the young man's name was Tim, they talked about the various qualities of womanhood, and how well you could decorate

13

these creatures with all the best that money could buy.

"It always seems to be" concluded Tim, as the train pulled into Southampton Central and he fought with his large anorak, "that such lovely stuff has an enormous price stuck to it, and it's always written in the smallest letters or numbers."

Hector shook hands with Tim. "Perhaps it's simply a matter of principle that if you need to know the price before buying, then already you can't afford it!"

Tim joined the crowd mauling their way off the train and waved as he passed Hector. Hector felt that here, at least, there was some hope for the future generations, if they could converse reasonably, and without the need to revert to the standard swearing vocabulary.

The train motored on through the New Forest, which Hector hadn't seen for a while and was delighted to see once more. He passed the time by spotting the forest ponies, which were sheltering from the cold weather under the forest canopy. Here and there a rabbit darted out from a hedgerow, scared witless by the sudden rushing-by of the train. After running in a panicky figure of eight, the rabbits would retreat to the warmth of their warren.

Half an hour later, the train arrived at Bournemouth, and Hector stepped from the train, having been given a shove of impatient encouragement from the group of travellers behind him. The suitcase smacked against someone's shin, and they yelled at him. He merely smiled, apologised for the bad manners of his luggage, and concentrated on the matter in hand of spotting Bob and Vicky in the crowd of meeters and greeters. They would surely be at the station to collect him.

A full forty-seven minutes later and Hector's temper was bristling to be unleashed. Of course, he held it at bay and continued his vigil for Bob or Vicky, for it would be stunning to see either of them at this point. He had aimed for the small café on the platform once it had initially become apparent that neither of his friends was there. Some refreshment would help pass the time and keep him warm, so he joined the queue which slowly made its way past perspex cases of cakes, filled rolls and sticky buns with Santa faces on them, all as if it was a vigil at Lenin's tomb.

The girl behind the large steaming and hissing urn looked blankly at him. "Do you have green tea?" he asked.

"No, Tetley's," mumbled the girl. Without giving further chance to consider the option, she slid a small stainless-steel teapot and milk jug across the table to him, motioned towards a stack of cups and saucers, and, with a scratch of her armpit, returned to sit at the cashier's till.

He picked up the teapot, which he found was so scalding hot it

14

could have been used by the British as a secret weapon in the Gulf Wars. Juggling it briefly, he scalded himself before letting go and sending a puddle of hot, dark tea off to discover the corners of the floor around the food cabinets. Picking up a bottle of mineral water, he gave the girl at the till a pound, waited for change which didn't come, and sat down as far away from his beverage fallout area as he could.

Another fifteen minutes crawled by, and, having squeezed the most he could out of a pound, he went in search of a payphone. With no sign of Bob or Vicky, or their Volvo estate car, he managed to pummel a coin into a public phone with all his concentrated strength, and called to find out where the happy couple were. As he stood in the telephone call box waiting for the line to dial out Bob and Vicky's number, he spied Bob speeding down the station ramp in the Volvo, and swinging round to a halt in the car park near the main entrance, not far from where he now stood, which he had suddenly realised doubled up both as a telephone box as well as an alternative solution for a public toilet.

He pushed his shoulder against the door of the call box, swung out of it, and turned a semicircle, aided by the momentum of his swinging suitcase. He dropped the suitcase on the kerbside, and began flapping his arms in Bob and Vicky's direction with an ever increasing urgency.

"There he is," said Vicky, who felt thrilled at having spotted an ex-pat whirling dervish on the forecourt of the station two days before Christmas. She exchanged glances with Bob, in the same way as couples who have been married for years tend to do. Not exactly telepathy, but there is that 'kind of knowing' that connects between souls. "You have to tell him now, before we get home, otherwise he'll be expecting full-on five-star Christmas cheer, and that's simply not right, now, is it?" she said over the top of her collar, which had been zipped right up, and which helped mask the faint odour of dark cream sherry.

Bob squirmed in his seat, and tried to cover it with the act of trying to release himself from the clutches of the Volvo's seatbelt. Feeling another glance from Vicky burn into him, he knew that what had to be done could not be delayed any longer. He climbed out of the car, leaving the engine running so Vicky could keep warm, and walked across the car park to where Hector had now stopped flapping and whirling, and was chuckling away to himself like a schoolboy who's just been told that 'bum' is a really rude word.

"Well, that certainly got the circulation going again in my veins. I hope you've got a hip flask of malt, or a secret stash hidden in that tank of yours – my system's just realised it's not in Singapore now," said Hector, in what sounded to Bob like one long and unpunctuated sentence, without pause for breath.

"Actually, we've got some sherry. Vicky's taking care of it for you now. Listen, Hector, there's some news we've got to tell you, now, before the Chris . . . "

Hector broke in. "Oh, God! Is she here? There won't be any sherry left now. Look at the car – the windows are all steamed up already. She's probably sat there as warm as toast, and can't wait to get a jab in at old Hector."

On that note, he let out two short dry coughs, and Bob took advantage. Grabbing Hector by the shoulders with both hands, Bob steadied himself, shifted weight from one foot to the other, and carried on from where he had been interrupted. "My dear friend, the most awful thing . . . "

"What's happened?" whispered Hector, still grinning from ear to ear. "Has the turkey run away before ma'am over there could have her bit of fun with the cleaver?"

Bob hoped that Vicky had saved some of the sherry. "It's Thomas. . . ."

"Oh, finally!" puffed out Hector. "How nice of him to show up at long last. Where's the bugger been hiding from me?"

Bob thought for a moment, and decided that to such a question as this, Christmas or not, a straight answer was all one could give to someone like Hector. After all, he'd appreciate it without all the fuss and froth. "He's lying in the mortuary," said Bob with hardly any expression on his face.

Hector straightened himself up, looked into the early evening sky, sniffed the crisp cold air, and repeated the words slowly. "The mortuary – that's bloody typical of him. I come all this way, and even bring a half-decent present for him this time, and the sod still manages to upstage me by snuffing it?"

"I'm afraid so," said Bob quietly. Holding onto Hector, Bob continued, safe in the knowledge that he had Hector's avid attention, although it was disconcerting to see the colour flow away from Hector's face, and it take on the look of having been pinched to bits by the winter weather. "I only wish I had been able to reach you sooner, but given the circumstances, it was down to me to liaise with the police, and at least to be there for Thomas' sake until you arrived."

Hector exhaled loudly, as if he had been holding his breath for the last couple of minutes. "What happened to him? Where, and how?" Hector's mind raced through reels of questions all at the same time, and he was glad of Bob's firm grip to keep a solid hold on him.

Bob continued: "He was staying further down the coast, and was about to make moves to get back here for you, he really did want to see you, but when they found him – the police were called, and took over. They found a note of my number and address in his wallet, and so it was me and Vicky who got the call. There's not really much you can

16

say when it happens. I mean, you think you would know, that you'd have it all worked out logically. But, when it actually happens, your mouth dries up, and your mind goes blank. Apart from wondering when you were exactly due to arrive, and knowing that I couldn't reach you, there was not much I could do. Anyway, seeing as we met up from time to time so I could give him the mail your secretary had sent to us for him, it was the trail that led the police to us by way of being 'the link' if you like."

The two friends looked deeply at each other. One stunned and rooted to the spot, the other keen to show support both physically as well as emotionally, yet, at the same time, somewhat eager to get all this nasty business off his chest. Not that anything malicious or evil had resulted in the death of Thomas, the post mortem had revealed a massive blockage to the heart – one of those things that healthy people on daytime television refer to as a 'time bomb' or even 'a heart attack waiting to happen'. Anyway, Bob didn't want to go into any unpleasant details at this point, so carefully, with his hand placed underneath Hector's elbow for steerage, they made their way across to the Volvo, where Vicky sat waiting, turning off the radio as Bob opened the car door for Hector, and guiding him into the rear passenger seat behind Vicky, where Hector was afforded the perfect view of her tightly curled Christmas hairdo.

"It's more of a hair-don't really," said Hector to himself.

"Pardon?" said Vicky.

"It doesn't matter," he replied. "I was just wondering who was going to get Thomas's present now." With that, a tear crept out of the corner of an eye, rippled over some wrinkles, and trickled down his cheek. Having forged a path, more tears followed, and he held up a hand to shield his face from the sad look that Bob now gave him through the rear-view mirror. The Volvo exited the station in a slightly more subtle manner than it had arrived, and together, with Vicky passing a plastic beaker of sherry over her shoulder to Hector, the car made its way through the town centre towards home, and the Christmas holidays that, this year, would introduce a few more surprises than usual.

Chapter Two

A View from the Shore

Bob and Hector sat at the kitchen table while Vicky fussed around them making tea, popping open cake tins, and arranging mince pies on a plate in front of them. Since arriving home at Bob and Vicky's Victorian three-storey house in a quiet and leafy area of Bournemouth, which had the added bonus of being a short walk downhill to the beach, not much had been said. What had filled the air more than anything was Vicky's scuttling, sniffing, and artificially jovial chatter, which rambled off into the darkness and left Hector bereft of tolerance, and trying to cling onto his air of colonial decency and stiff upper lip.

Bob fidgeted, indicating how uncomfortable he was about the whole scenario. "Until the post-mortem has been carried out, the police won't release Thomas for a funeral, and that means that nothing can get moving until between Christmas and New Year." Bob looked hard at Hector, checking for some sign that what he had just said was being absorbed. "Mr Harper is one of the best funeral directors in the town, and has done a couple of Vicky's family over recent years, hasn't he, love? I'm sure he'll take good care of Thomas for you."

Vicky sank her teeth into a mince pie, which immediately gave up the fight, collapsed in on itself and scattered all over the table. "Bugger!" she muttered quietly to herself. "Mr Harper? Yes, he was very good, and never in a hurry. Always a good listener. Let's face it, if you're going to be in that business, you need to be a good listener, don't you?" Pouring out three cups of strong, piping-hot tea, Vicky did an exchange of glances with Bob, passed the cups round, and scooped up the remains and crumbs from the table in the aftermath of the mince pie's suicide. Offering the plate of pies, cake and biscuits to Hector, Vicky enquired with a higher pitch than normal, "Bikky, dear?"

He dismissed the offer with a wave of his hand, blew hard on the surface of the tea, and slurped a mouthful. "It's so cold. I know that sounds like stating the obvious for this time of year, but I wasn't aware of just how cold it would be, and that includes indoors as well as outdoors."

Bob thought briefly, and then said, "It's probably the shock too. We just thought that, before anything got festively out of hand, we had a duty to give you the news. We're sorry if it didn't come across as subtly as we hoped, but, when you're telling someone about a death, subtlety rarely gets a chance to lessen the weight of such heavy words."

"No, it's fine, really," said Hector, who had finished his tea in about four gulps. "I just want to go to bed and be on my own for a bit. We'll talk more in the morning, see if we can speak to the police and have a chat with this fellow Harper. But, for now, just give me some space, okay?" He stood up, as if to underline the intention of his words.

Bob nodded, and Vicky hurtled out of the kitchen uttering, "Bugger! Bugger! Bugger!" rapid-fire, whilst she tore up the stairs to the airing cupboard, pulled a bath towel out and put it at the end of the bed in the spare room. She passed Hector on the stairs with the air of a secret agent in a James Bond movie. "On the end of your bed, Hector – towel."

Not knowing what to say at times of distress for others, Vicky had always resorted to the school of thought that life, as well as the show, must go on. Hence, very little emotion of any sort ever made an appearance, and it was easy to misread her.

Hector took a deep breath, remembering this. "Thank you, dear," he said. "I'll come down in my own time for breakfast in the morning."

"No trouble at all," bluffed Vicky.

Closing the door, he undressed himself, hung most of his clothes over an Edwardian chair next to the bed, and, pulling the blankets up to his chin, lay in the dark wondering how long it would be before his feet regained their feeling; how much he would detest being brought a cup of tea in bed first thing in the morning; and why had the police deemed it necessary to hold a post-mortem on Thomas's body.

As the daylight streaked through the curtains, Hector stirred in his bed and turned over to face the bedside table, on top of which rested a cold cup of tea. Seeing that the time was after nine, he shaved whilst sitting in the bath, got dressed, and presented himself downstairs in the kitchen to the deafening sound of silence that indicated he had been the topic of discussion.

"I've spoken to the police, and the funeral director," Bob said to the sugar bowl. "Apparently, no suspicious circumstances, so Mr Harper said we can lay him to rest on the 30th."

With that said, Bob put a plate of bacon and eggs in front of Hector, and filled a mug with hot, dark tea. Vicky dried her hands on a tea towel, and checked the fridge for stock replacement.

"Did you manage to get some sleep, Hector?" she said in what was becoming an increasingly irritating sing-song tone of voice.

He nodded, finished his breakfast, and stood in the hallway putting on his overcoat. "I think I'll take a walk along the seafront for a while. You don't mind if I just have some time to clear my head and get used to things, do you?"

"Not at all," cooed Vicky. "Bob and I will go to the supermarket, won't we, Bob."

This was more of a statement than a question, and Bob shrugged his shoulders in acceptance of things he couldn't change. He wanted to go for a walk by the beach too, but understood his friend's craving for solitude.

Bob and Vicky drove off in the Volvo towards town, with Hector heading in the other direction downhill to the beach.

The air was fresh and bracing, and, across the sky, clouds were limply hanging about waiting for the winter weather to wreak some seasonal havoc. The beach and promenade were bare, except for an elderly woman being taken for a walk along the sand by her apricot-coloured poodle. The dog was tightly wrapped in a tartan doggie jacket, and the woman was well protected against the elements by a plastic rain hood and winter coat. Hector correctly assessed that it was her intention that the dog should be the one to get some exercise before being stuffed with goodies on Christmas Day. The dog had other ideas, and consequently was having a lovely time making his mistress wheeze and cough her way along the beach.

Walking past the rows of beach huts, which were shut up for the winter, he presently arrived at a bench and sat down for a while. The bench had a small plaque screwed into it, dedicating the spot 'In memory of Aunt Beryl, who loved this place'. He had to agree with Aunt Beryl, the view across the beach to the sea, and the headland that curled around the bay to his right, was beautiful. There was something about the open view that gave him the time to think about things: his brother, the impending funeral, and Christmas.

As much as he adored Singapore, Hector found the spot by the beach quite liberating. The sheer space around him was a luxury compared to being in the midst of a bustling Singapore, and he realised that he ought to try to contact Jean. She should be told, and, besides, it probably meant that he would have to stay in England longer than first anticipated. No time for Ireland now, so that would have to wait until another opportunity presented itself.

. He pondered on past memories with Thomas – their many childhood adventures, being scared to pieces by Thomas's never-ending practical jokes, and the shared teenage laughter over jokes that parents didn't catch – and then the distance that Thomas had put between himself and Hector in their adult years. He had always made excuses for not being able to go to Singapore, no matter how well Jean had decorated the invitation. He only called Hector when he needed money, and he was full of gushing words that promised a drink and chat when they next met up. Sadly, this had never fully realised the potential reacquaintance of the two brothers. The only time Hector had shared a meal and drink with his brother in recent memory had been at the wedding a year and a half before. Since weddings tend to be occasions when invited guests try to be on their best behaviour, he felt, as always, that these events were always the wrong place to try to get an angle on people's characters. Alcohol and rich food always managed to cloud over real emotions, merely tending to intensify the less important feelings people had. As a result, Hector had found himself in the middle of some tight situations – arguments and fights – that he would rather have avoided. Such had been the case at the wedding where he had met Thomas for the last time, and, whilst he had been at length to extract himself from the brewing pot of drink-fuelled atmosphere, it had been Thomas who had defused tearful women, and asserted himself as top dog among the loud group of men at the bar.

Hector felt a smack of cold wind come rushing at him from the sea, and, seeing how long he had been sat thinking, he got up, thanked Aunt Beryl for her legacy, and walked back to Bob and Vicky's. Whereupon, entering the hall and hearing the shouting and panic coming from the kitchen, it dawned on Hector that this was now Christmas Eve. Vicky would be in full catering flow in the kitchen, and Bob had been harnessed into support by way of preparing vegetables for Christmas Day's onslaught of food.

Hector groaned and crept upstairs, quietly removing his coat as he went and, deftly shutting the door behind him, lay on the bed in his room for a brief rest from the evolving hurricane downstairs. Weathermen always gave funny names to hurricanes the world over, so 'Vicky' seemed rather apt to him, by way of describing the disaster about to happen with Bob and a stuffed turkey in the kitchen. Bob would eventually calm things down, and all would return to a more normal pace, so Hector drifted off to sleep comforted by this thought.

A couple of hours later, he sleepily came downstairs to hear Vicky muttering, "Bugger!" at having run out of mince pies, and rushing from lounge to kitchen with an empty plate, leaving Bob to cope with a room full of neighbours, who had been invited in for the evening.

"Oh! You're home, then, dear?" Vicky said as she juggled with a hot baking tray being wrestled from the oven. "Everyone's in the lounge for drinks and nibbles before tomorrow, so go on in and join them. It'll do you good."

Hector was sure that it wouldn't, but didn't have time to evade Vicky's glowing face. Finding himself linked by one of her cardigan-clad arms, he was pulled into the lounge to face a room full of strangers, who had all been warned about the man from Singapore, and his current state of affairs with a recently deceased brother.

Bob passed Hector a glass of sherry, and Vicky piled a paper plate full of canapés along with the best nibbles that the supermarket could produce this year.

Sitting in the middle of the sofa, Hector gingerly balanced the paper plate on his knee, sipped the sherry, and listened to everyone's stories about life in Bournemouth, and where they were going for the annual Christmas morning pilgrimage to seek out six-course lunches from families they hardly saw from one year to the next.

After what seemed like an eternity to him, he felt overpowered by stomach cramps and wind, due to the fact that eating nibbles in a confined space wasn't to be recommended. He took advantage of a pause in conversation, and whispered a goodnight to Bob.

He sat by the window in his room and observed partygoers making their exit from Vicky's soirée, snaking their way down the path out into the street, and clashing with a pack of younger party people returning from a disco in town. The confusion was noisy but jocular, and it took several minutes for people to untangle themselves from one another.

Hector smiled at the scene, and, hearing Bob and Vicky coming upstairs, he got into the icebox of a bed he had just about got used to. He thanked his lucky stars for having had the foresight at C. K. Tang's to buy some thick socks, since it helped warm his toes against the tundra conditions at the foot of the bed.

Christmas morning arrived glistening with frost. Some kind individual had written swear words with his finger all over the windscreen of Bob and Vicky's Volvo, which was parked outside in the street. Here and there a small child screamed with ecstasy as he hurtled along the pavement on board a freshly unwrapped bicycle or, in one case, a skateboard. The couple from two doors away were already loading up their car with bags full of gifts, and, after a short while, sped away up the hill in hot pursuit of a cousin in Somerset.

Bob was already in the kitchen, having set the alarm clock for six in order to load the turkey into the oven. The two friends wished each other a merry Christmas, and had a small bowl of cereal, seeing how, as Bob put it, "Vicky's prepared lunch for half the county."

As if on cue, Vicky shuffled into the kitchen with what looked like the symptoms of a huge hangover. "It must have been something I ate last night. I feel terrible," she mumbled to all and nobody. With that, she dropped two aspirins into a glass tumbler of water, and stirring it hurriedly, sat down at the kitchen table clutching her dressing gown across her bosom.

Bob tendered a plate of buttered toast on the table in front of Vicky. "Eat this," he said softly. "You'll feel much better with something inside you. Talking of which, the stuffing finally set last night, so I've done the bird, and it's been sitting on the middle shelf in the oven since six o'clock." Bob felt quietly pleased with himself.

Vicky tested a couple of bites of toast, swigged the fizzing aspirin down in one, and, with all her mustered energy, rose from the kitchen table. She briefly exchanged a weak smile with Hector, left the kitchen and climbed the stairs, bathroom-bound, to prepare herself for the day ahead. "Thank God the veg is done," was all that could be coherently heard from her mouth as the bathroom door closed behind her.

"I don't know what gets into her sometimes," said Bob as he and Hector took cutlery, napkins, and a box of crackers from next to the bread bin, and wandered into the dining room, which lead off the lounge through some double doors. "I can't decide if it's hostess nerves, or if she feels that she owes it to herself to get the party going, takes over, and goes through the sound barrier."

Hector paused in front of the dining table. "How many are coming for lunch? You've given me four sets of knives and forks to lay."

"Ah, well," Bob said to the toy robin and plastic holly decoration that sat in the middle of the table. "We invited Bernie over for lunch, you see. This was all planned before we knew about Thomas. To be honest, Bernie doesn't have much on for most of the year, so Vicky said we should do the Christian thing for Christmas and cater for four, rather than three. You don't mind, do you? Bernie's no trouble, and always manages to entertain."

Hector set about his task of laying the cutlery at table. "No, I don't mind," he sighed. "After all, there's no point in our sitting around the table for Christmas lunch as if it were a seance or something, is there? I'm sure it'll be fine – delightful even – and, if what you say is true, I'll look forward to having the entertainment of a lunch guest to help take my mind off Thomas." He reassured himself that it really would be fine, and, by the time he and Bob had finished, the table looked a treat.

"Where did you learn to do the napkins like that?" said Bob as he admired the creations that floated in wine glasses as if they would take off shortly and escort the robin on three laps around the Christmas tree.

"Tokyo," replied Hector. "Rather a lot of patience is needed, never mind the etiquette, when dealing for pearls and such things with one's Japanese clients. As I recall, it was a karaoke bar, around three in the morning, and let's say there was an exchange of cultural affairs. They taught me how to do things like this with napkins, and I taught them the words to several Irish songs by The Dubliners. It seemed a fair trade at the time, and I got the pearls."

Bob took his glasses off, breathed on them, and rubbed them with his handkerchief. "We move in totally different circles, Hector. The nearest I get to cultural exchanges is sharing betting tips with Mr Kapoor at the newsagents."

By the time Vicky came downstairs, Bob and Hector were chuckling together in the kitchen, taking turns at peeking through the glass oven door at the turkey, and about to start their third glass of port and brandy.

"Don't start the party without me, boys," Vicky squealed. The aspirins, and a long spell in the bathroom had worked their tricks, and it was plain to see that she was crusading forth for a day to remember.

The front doorbell rang and, at the same time, the telephone cried out to be answered. Vicky bustled to the door, throwing it open with one hand, and picking up the phone with the other.

"Merry Christmas!" she boomed.

Bernie crossed the doorstep with the words, "I reckon Herod had a point, you know: those bloody kids have dive-bombed me from all directions down the road." With that, she sailed down the hallway and swept into the kitchen, where she firmly planted a wicker shopping basket, full of gift-wrapped bottles, on the table, inspected Bob, and then checked herself at having come face-to-face with Hector.

Vicky's head poked round the kitchen door. "It's for you, Hector – someone in Singapore. They've already had their Christmas Day, and eight hours ahead they are. Fancy that! It's boiling hot there too. Not really Christmas, is it? All that heat and stickiness. Have you basted the turkey, Bob?"

Hector bowed slightly to Bernie, and strode to the phone. "Hector Barnes speaking," he said as he turned and perched on the lower part of the staircase.

"Merry Christmas, Hector. Has Vicky ever worked for Israeli intelligence? She ought to, given the number of questions I've just had. I just wanted to give you a greeting, and to see how you are." It was Jean.

"You don't know how glad I am to hear your voice," he said quietly. "Everything started off okay, but when Bob and Vicky met me at the station, they told me that Thomas had died suddenly, in a guest house somewhere." The delay in the satellite echoed his voice, so that Hector heard his words repeated.

"Oh! How awful for you! I don't know what to say, my dear. Is there anything I can do for you from here?"

Although he could tell from the tone of her voice that she was upset for him, Hector drew comfort from the simple fact that it was a familiar and reassuring voice talking to him, and the distance between them seemed unimportant. "Well, the funeral's booked in for the 30th, apparently. Bob and Vicky have been very good. Needless to say, I shan't be going to Ireland for the New Year, and, as much as I think about putting it off, I'm sure there are affairs of his to be sorted. Could you call the airlines and cancel my return flight? I don't know when I'll be ready to come home yet."

Jean waited for the echo to bounce, and then continued: "Consider it done. At least you've got a flexible ticket. Shall I send flowers? I've got Bob and Vicky's address here, next to their phone number."

That was typical of Jean. No matter where he was in the world, she always knew how to get hold of him. She had tried for months to get Hector to have a mobile phone, but he had held out on that one. He hated them.

"I think not to the flowers. A big bushel of orchids will seem over the top, compared to the selections I've seen on display around here." Suddenly, something else dawned on him. "Why aren't you in Australia or New Zealand, as I suggested?"

There was a pause.

"Have you tried getting a seat going in that direction at the last minute a week before Christmas? I gave up in the end, got some nice treats in, have had a couple of friends from the embassy over, and they left about an hour ago. So, you see, I'm fine. Besides, you're the important one at the moment. Thank goodness I called. When were you going to tell me?"

Hector shifted his weight about, as his buttocks were getting numb on the stairs. "I know. I meant to do so earlier. I thought about it yesterday while I was looking out to sea. You crossed my mind then."

Jean waited a moment. "Looking out to sea? I trust that's as far as you went, Hector. Anyway, all is well here at the office. Even Alex is quieter than he usually is. I think he misses you more than he'd care to admit to. Don't worry about the place, I can put your meetings back, and delay the Italians with their jewellery designs and orders. They'll understand, being Catholics."

Hector felt eyes on him, and looked over his shoulder to see Vicky and Bernie's heads disappear back into the kitchen. He concluded to

Jean, "I'm doing all right. They're trying their best to keep me occupied. I've known Bob long enough to know that he's there for me when the chips are down. Indeed, as you are. I'll try to call you after the funeral, and we'll catch up then. I can smell turkey roasting in the oven, and I can't leave Bob alone with the company we've got for lunch."

"Okay. Well, know that I'm here for you, whatever. Enjoy your lunch, and have a couple of whiskies for me. Goodbye, dear."

With that, the call finished, but not before Hector swore he could have heard a compact clip shut via the echo on the phone.

Back in the kitchen, Hector negotiated Bernie's larger-than-life chest, and squeezed his way towards the port and brandy. He had been taken aback for a moment when Bernie had descended on the household. For some reason, it had been male company he had expected. The name Bernie conjured up images of Lancashire-based long-distance lorry drivers, or retired Birmingham carpet salesmen. As it unfolded, Bernie was short for Bernadette, who originally hailed from Cork. She had done a stint as an Aer Lingus flight attendant during the seventies, and had married a pottery manager from Poole, who brought her to the south coast. They had enjoyed a happy marriage for nearly twenty years, whereupon the angels had called for him, and his time was up, as she told Hector over melon and Parma ham.

"Since then, it's been pretty bog-standard – just the yoga classes that I team up and suffer with Vicky, and the annual summer visit back home to an ever increasing family of cousins, nephews and nieces, and the few old ones that are left. You know what I mean."

Hector didn't know at all. After all those years in Singapore, not an ounce of family growth had occurred on his patch, just the simple decline of it in England. There had been a couple of long-term affairs, which had matured into stable relationships. But then, as had always been the case, the gem emporium had reminded him that it reigned supreme as the true mistress in his life. With his trips all over the world, sometimes lengthy, the ladies in Singapore had got bored and moved on.

"Such is life," he said, as Vicky brought the turkey in triumphantly. She ordered Bob to remove the robin and holly to make room for the feast. "After all," said Hector, "that fellow was running around last week without a care in the world, and now look at him!"

Bernie raised her glass. "A toast to my friends. Thanks for having me at your table; and, for absent friends, turkey included, wish you were here."

Nervous laughter quivered around the table, except for Bernie, who smacked her lips and prepared to tuck into the plate of food, which Bob placed in front of her with much ceremony.

After eating more than was good for them, which most people do at Christmas time, everyone adjourned to the comfort of the lounge. Vicky stacked all the dishes, plates and bowls in the kitchen, and made a mental note to remind Bob that the washing-up should be done before any of the remains that were left on the plates could go hard.

She made it to the sofa in time for the Queen's Christmas broadcast to the nation, and laughed when Hector stood up for the national anthem.

"Nobody does that any more, dear. Even the cinemas have stopped playing it after films. My God, you've been away from this country for far too long."

Hector sat down embarrassed, flushed with a streak of hot anger, and contemplated several lethal methods of torture for Vicky's hair. "It's a great shame that people don't stand for the anthem as they used to. We have a sovereign who is known the world over, and envied by nearly every republic for the figurehead status she holds, and the love, respect, and income she generates for the country. She is one of the best things that Britain puts out to attract tourists, and, on the home front, when things get tough, people still look to her for assurance."

Bob fidgeted in his armchair. Bernie downed her glass of port, and went off in search of a fresh bottle from the wicker basket.

Vicky sniffed. "Yes, well, just look at her," she spat. "Looks done in and exhausted, she does, not to mention much older. It's no wonder, given the rest of the Royal family and their antics this year."

At this, Hector decided it would be prudent to save any further remarks for another time. He wasn't going to start a row over the monarchy today. Besides, Bernie had just returned with a refilled glass of port, and had peeped round the lounge door before entering, as if to check the need for armour before making herself comfortable on the sofa again.

It wasn't long before they had all dozed off, aided by the rest of Bernie's port, a box of chocolates shared between the four of them, and the film on television, which they had all seen about five times over the years.

The day was rounded off by a procession of more food on the trolley, which Vicky wheeled into the lounge and dished out onto paper plates.

"At least that will save Bob more washing-up," said Bob as he bit into a stick of celery.

Bernie made moves to leave around ten. Swathed in her bright-red pashmina, she hugged and kissed all. Stroking Hector's cheek, she said, "I'm so sorry for your loss. I hope today hasn't been too over the top from how you wanted it to be. If you need an extra arm for support, I'll come to the funeral with you."

He sighed. "That's very decent of you, but I think I'll be okay. Thank you for your company today, though. It's meant a lot, and made the day pass with many smiles. It's nice to have your Irish charm and humour around."

Bernie laughed, and set forth down the front path with Bob in her wake. He had decided that she should be escorted home, even though it was just to the top of the road, and more for the sake of anyone they encountered on the way.

Boxing Day passed quietly in the house. Cold rain threw itself at the ground furiously, and the wind made sure it wasn't to be left out of the show. Hector spent most of the morning in his room, keen to have some time to get his mind set for the funeral, and whatever would follow it. Though Bob had been the one to liaise with Mr Harper, and make all the arrangements, Hector wondered and amazed himself with the thought that, when all was said and done, he didn't know the grown-up Thomas at all. As the rain splintered off the window, he realised that he would need to start thinking in the past tense from now on whenever his brother came to mind. It had all been a terrible shock.

The day of the funeral dawned with the sound of Bob having a stop-start pee in the toilet, so Hector, who had endured an endless night of interrupted sleep, which seemed to mirror Bob's bladder at this point in time, got up, went downstairs to the kitchen and put the kettle on.

Bob came into the kitchen, and holding out his hand said, "I thought you may need this. It's not something I would have imagined you packed when you left Singapore."

Hector accepted the black tie, and replied, "You certainly got that right. Can I just say, before the day gets under way, how grateful I am to you for everything that you've done for me. This country seems so alien to me. It's different from being in London for a day or two to have meetings with South African diamond people. I thought it would be the same feeling, and type of place, but it isn't."

"Don't mention it," Bob said to the teapot as he filled it from the kettle. "We'll get through today just fine. I've even put my foot down, and told Vicky to be quiet as much as she can. She means well, Hector, she just isn't very good at expressing herself."

On this point, he had to agree.

They had breakfast, got dressed, managed to prise Vicky from the bathroom before too much time had been lost for the men to shave, and were all sat in the lounge when Mr Harper knocked at the door.

Shaking Hector's hand, he offered his sincerest sympathy in a well-rehearsed, and almost overused turn of phrase.

Vicky pulled the curtains in the lounge, reminding Bob that she'd done it out of respect for Thomas, and then led the way out to the waiting car that then set off behind the hearse, wound its way through town, and presently arrived at the crematorium.

"Nothing we can do about the traffic, I'm afraid," said Mr Harper. "Most folks are at the sales, and, when that happens, it clogs up the town with frustrated couples trying to find parking spaces. Still, we made it on time."

With that, he ushered Hector, Bob and Vicky from the car into the waiting area next to the chapel, where another service was just ending.

To Hector's surprise, there were about twenty people waiting for Thomas, most of whom looked rather dubious and suspect to him. He knew that Thomas was – no, had been – an antique dealer, and had travelled backwards and forwards all over the country, buying goods at salerooms, auctions and car boot sales, and then selling them on via his network of contacts that stretched from Plymouth to Aberdeen. It would seem that these people were a representation of Thomas's world. How was it that there were always more people than you expected at a funeral? Moreover, how they all found out about the proceedings and appeared out of nowhere was beyond him.

Mr Harper approached, almost apologetically, and whispered that they were ready. So, with that, people filed into the chapel, and almost in unison, all had a good look at Hector as he took his seat in the front pew.

Vicky sat down and pulled her coat tightly around her, resisting the temptation to remark that, considering it was a crematorium, it was bloody, buggery freezing.

The vicar said some words, welcoming everyone, and directed them to the leaflets that were in the pews, which contained the order of service, along with words to the chosen hymns.

Hector didn't need any prompting with the words to hymns, as both he and Thomas had sung with gusto at school all those years before. Even in Singapore, Hector attended the Church of England services at St Andrew's for Easter, Harvest Festival and, of course, Christmas. Now, here he was, immediately after Christmas, attending his brother's funeral with a pack of total strangers, except for Bob and Vicky.

Everyone stood, and began singing 'Abide with Me'.

Above all else, Hector's voice could be heard singing to the point of almost shouting. 'Predictable but dependable,' he thought to himself about the hymn. 'Hopefully, they'll know this one.'

They did, and, on sitting down again after the hymn, people began to feel not so much strangers to one another. Nothing was said, but you could tell that this was the point at which they all realised they were there to say farewell to Thomas, and that in future, they would be able to beat the sly old goat to all the best trappings at the salerooms and auctions.

The vicar gave a brief synopsis of Thomas's life, based on what Bob and Hector had told him. He mentioned Thomas's brother Hector, who had come from Singapore for the funeral, which, although not exactly true, prompted someone to whisper from the back of the chapel, "Oh, so that's who it is!"

They sang 'The Lord Is My Shepherd', and, with prayers and reflection in full flow, Thomas's coffin departed, sending him over the horizon into the next world, and onto a higher plain.

Hector, the vicar and Bob all stood at the door while people passed out of the chapel, shaking hands, saying how sorry they were, what a great ball of fun Thomas had been, and was there food and drink on offer afterwards? There wasn't.

It was while Vicky was half in and half out of the car, with Bob holding the car door with one hand and her handbag with the other, that a small man with greasy hair and yellow teeth trotted over to Hector. "Mr Barnes? Mr Hector Barnes?"

Hector eyed the man up and down, and acknowledged the fact that indeed, he was Thomas's brother.

"Oh, good!" said the small man. "Well, I don't mean that about today's event, but I was told by your brother some time ago that, other than flying to Singapore, this would be the place where I would be sure to find you. I've never been fond of long-haul flying; Alicante is quite enough for me once a year, thank you very much," he chuckled.

"Exactly who are you, and what can I do for you?" said Hector flatly, feeling his patience waning, and, being aware of Vicky doing her best to eavesdrop, indicated that they should take a few steps away from the waiting car.

Mr Harper nodded that there was no hurry, or at least that they had a few minutes before the next batch of bereaved would arrive.

"I'm sorry, Mr Barnes. My name is Newman, Neil Newman. I was your brother's solicitor."

This came as a surprise, as, up until this point, Hector had fancied that the man looked like a racecourse bookie. A solicitor would have been the last thing he would have thought of. "I see. So is there a problem of some sort?"

Hector was prepared for a large bill of some sort that Thomas had run up, and which needed settlement. 'Here it comes,' he thought as he saw Mr Newman produce an envelope from his jacket pocket.

"Several years ago, your brother decided it was as right a time as any to make a will. That will is in the safe at my office, and I am instructed to hold it there, pending your reading of this letter and subsequent actions." As an afterthought, feeling the need to state the obvious, Mr Newman sucked back some spittle in his mouth, and said, "It's from your brother, Mr Barnes. My address and phone number are on the back of the envelope, so I'll expect to hear from you when you are good and ready."

Hector looked at the envelope, put it in his pocket, and, on looking up, saw Mr Newman scuttling off as if in a hurry to get away before anyone recognised him.

"How strange!" Hector said as he climbed into the car. After looking at Bob, and saying that he was perfectly all right, they set off back to the house, where, after thanking Mr Harper for his service and efforts, Hector retired to his room. Sitting on the bed, he opened the envelope and read the following letter from Thomas:

Hector,

I know that reading this letter you will either have just attended my funeral, or Neil has taken tranquillisers and flown to Singapore to hand this to you. Knowing Neil as I do, I'll hedge my bets on the funeral story. Don't be put off by him, he's a good sort, sharp as a knife, and knows his stuff. Above all, he's trustworthy, and, writing this, I know he will not let me down. He will give you this, which I want you to digest, and try to follow.

It would seem that, as we have got older, we have grown apart. There's no recrimination in that, simply that Singapore isn't exactly down the road for me. Your visits to England have always been so rushed, and, for the most part, limited to London. I wish there had been more time for us to get to know each other again. Yes, I know you have offered many a time to give me a ticket to come over and see you, or rather your secretary has offered on your behalf. Along with the birthday and Christmas cards, which she has also sent with regular efficiency, it has been very impressive, and could only have been bettered had any one of the cards or invitations come personally from you, preferably handwritten. No matter, I recognise that your intentions were genuine.

I have spent a long time running all over the country getting bargains, and sometimes not. But, I have always gone for quality. Knowing your trade, this would probably be the currently binding factor between us. We both know a good thing when we see it. Consequently, I have kept a rather nice 19th-century oriental tea caddy for you. It's made from boxwood, with rosewood inlay, and is the sort of thing I know you will enjoy having in your Singapore home. In order to collect it, though, you have to do something for me. I know you will think it's another of Thomas's practical jokes, and, believe me, maybe it would have been better for you had that been the case, but it really isn't. Nor is it any kind of trick. Think of it as a task and favour for me. The tea caddy will be yours to do with as you see fit, and to remind you of me, and that things of quality like us are not just made in the past. The present and future also hold the possibility for the creation of quality.

Please go to the following address and seek out Barbara. She will fill you in, and guide you to the next stage.

> *The Bide-a-Wee Guest House,*
> *27 Argyll Road,*
> *Boscombe.*

I have known Barbara for a long time, and by the same token she knows me inside out. I have told her of you, your life in the East, and the fact that the only time you would come back for any visit longer than usual would be to attend my funeral. She'll look after you. I would urge you to go as soon as you can, for no reason other than that, despite Bob's well-mannered and calming friendship, you will probably be more than happy to have a reason to leave Vicky's domain for a while.

In all these years, you have jumped in and out of my mind on a regular basis. Have I jumped in and out of yours? From now on, I retain the comfort that you will always think of me. Learn to relax, and to let yourself go from time to time. We only pass this way but once, so make the most of it. Do things you would ordinarily hesitate over or avoid altogether.

Be well and happy always,

Thomas.

Hector read the letter four times, and went in search of aspirin for the eruption of a headache he was getting.

Having slept deeply, and awoken the next morning, he filled Bob in on the letter, and asked where Boscombe was. Bob was more than happy to get his local AA road map from the Volvo. He pinpointed Argyll Road, which, much to Hector's relief, was located in a suburb on the other side of town, compared to the other side of the country, which he had been afraid of.

To be on the safe side, and for the practical reason of not lugging a large suitcase everywhere, Bob fished around in the cupboard under the stairs and produced an overnight bag, which Hector duly filled with his necessities.

Vicky appeared in the kitchen, her curiosity bringing her downstairs almost an hour sooner than usual. "Where are you off to?" she asked, trying hard not to sound nosey, but coming across at best as probing.

"Boscombe," said Hector. "There would appear to be something I have to take care of for Thomas, and, whilst I'm not overly surprised, I hope that it will not take too long."

Vicky scooped two heaped spoonfuls of sugar into her tea, and with one hand on her hip looked at the overnight bag on the floor, and back again to him. "Well, a change of scenery will probably do you good. I'm sure it will certainly give you that."

Bob came puffing through the front door. "Ready when you are," he said, followed swiftly by, "Morning, love. You're up early. I'm just going to run Hector across town. I won't be long."

Hector pecked Vicky on the cheek, and strode out to the car with Bob. Together they set off up the hill.

Having negotiated several one-way systems around the busy town centre, Bob brought the Volvo to a halt outside 27 Argyll Road, and, turning the engine off, looked up at the building through the windscreen.

Hector climbed out of the car and stood still for a moment, staring at the outside of the guest house. He wondered what Thomas had stored up his sleeve to surprise him with, as the mere fact that he had departed this life did not mean that Hector underestimated the capabilities of his brother.

Argyll Road was a fairly narrow side road, leading off from the main thoroughfare of Boscombe, in the more run-down part of the eastern suburbs of Bournemouth. At one point in its history, around the turn of the 20th century, it had been an important enough part of the resort town to warrant the construction of its own pier. Bournemouth had a rather grand pier, complete with a theatre at the end of it. Consequently, Boscombe was not one to be left out of the limelight, so councillors and townsfolk alike were delighted to have their own pier constructed. It was duly opened with much pomp and ceremony by the Duke of Argyll at a gala day celebration in 1889. Although Bournemouth felt they really held the upper hand for entertaining the holiday masses in the theatre on their pier, the townsfolk of Boscombe, perhaps feeling this to be a bit tacky, kept their standards flying with a bandstand on their pier, and entertained their visitors that way. Over the years, the suburb held on to a good selection of shops and arcades for people to meander around, and, whilst Bournemouth town centre had the larger shops and department stores, Boscombe had retained some character, and came to be known as a downsized version of Bournemouth. However, by the mid-eighties, an economic downturn, the ease with which people turned their holiday plans to overseas destinations, and the high running costs for almost anything, meant that Boscombe took a steep nosedive into the seedy side of British seaside resort life. The main road, which had once boasted a good selection of quality tailors, haberdashers and delicatessens, was now a run-down parade, tired and gutted. Most of the good shops had gone, only to be replaced by second-hand stores, a stream of antique shops, all of which had a somewhat unsavoury air about them, and, as seemed to be the case everywhere these days, a growing number of banks, building societies and estate agents, all fighting over the same number of clients and properties.

Hector looked up and down the road, feeling saddened by the sight of so many old homes, all in a state of semi-dereliction, or at least crying out for a good few thousand pounds worth of repairs to be done.

Bob retrieved the bag from the back seat of the car, and together they faced the front entrance of the guest house, which had a covered porch with a selection of spidery and straggling geranium plants on show. Underneath the doorbell was a handwritten note, Sellotaped several times in the past decade, but managing to keep its yellowy age guarantee in view for all, announcing the obvious, 'Ring for Attention'.

Both of them stood in the porch, staring at the bell and its label.

"I think I'd better handle it from here," said Hector, shaking hands with Bob. "If there's any emergency, I'll be in touch right away, but, from the look of this place, I can't imagine any emergency at all, can you?"

Bob couldn't, saying, "Not since the last war, I shouldn't think. Okay, then, I'll shoot off. I'll wait in the car before driving away, just in case nobody's at home. Once you're in, I'll be on my way back to Vicky."

All this sounded like a hushed escape plan from Colditz, as the two men were whispering to each other. Bob went back to the Volvo, climbed in and waited. Hector rang the doorbell, and then inspected his finger as if something highly contagious had just rubbed off onto it.

From behind the door, Hector could hear music and someone shouting, or was it singing? After a brief pause, the door opened and a small woman, with washing-up gloves on, removed the cigarette from the corner of her heavily lipsticked razor slash of a mouth, and looked up and down at the tall and distinguished-looking man in front of her.

. "I'm sorry, love. If you're looking for a room, we're not taking anyone in at the moment, what with it being New Year's Eve. I'm not washing vomit out of me carpets at seven tomorrow morning for nobody."

Hector cringed slightly at the notion that she should consider him in that category. "I'm looking for Barbara," he said with as little intonation as possible. This was as fierce-looking a female as he'd ever met, so he wasn't about to get on the wrong side of her.

"Well, you've found her. Who are you, anyway? Are you from the council? I've already told someone over the phone that the drains can't be dealt with until the holidays are over."

Hector coughed, and decided to deliver his pitch into the ring. "I have been directed to you by my brother, Thomas Barnes. He said I was to come and find you. Well, I have, and, despite it being New Year's Eve, I got the impression from his letter that you would be expecting me." With that, he took a small step back and waited.

Barbara puffed hard on her cigarette, removed the washing-up gloves, and beckoned for Hector to enter. "So you are Hector Barnes. All the way from Hong Kong. No, wait a minute, it was Singapore, wasn't it? Well, yes, you'd better come in. I'm sure we can fix a room up for you. You can tell your friend in the Volvo to go now. We've got a lot to discuss."

Looking round Hector's body, for she was too short to peep over his shoulder, Barbara waved at Bob. Hector turned, waved too, and Bob took the cue. He drove away bound for an evening of whisky, a haggis which had split in its pan of boiling-hot water, and Vicky's attempt to first-foot the home at the stroke of midnight, which would be highlighted by an incident with a dustbin and next door's cat.

The long hallway of the Bide-a-Wee was a slice of seventies' decor, untouched by a decorator's hand since the swirling wallpaper had first been pasted. The carpet was well worn, even bald in spots, but still managed to catch the eye thanks to its brown, red and orange bold pattern. Hector wondered what all the fuss had been about over some party-reveller's vomit spillage; you'd have a job to find it in that pattern.

Barbara called him from her living room, and he walked into what truly surpassed the hallway's first impression. The entire living room had been turned into some sort of shrine to Elvis Presley, with the King splattered everywhere. Barbara had poured two tumblers of Scotch, and was fishing around in a large plastic pineapple for ice cubes.

"Sit down anywhere, except that armchair over there. That's Bonnie's, and she doesn't take kindly to intruders."

Hector sat on a two-seater sofa, propped himself up with an Elvis cushion, and accepted the drink from Barbara. They sat in silence for a few minutes, sizing each other up, and thinking about what to say first, or even where to start.

Barbara lit a cigarette with an Elvis lighter, and, squinting out of one eye, took a long draw, and exhaled slowly. "So, Thomas is dead, is he?" she asked frankly.

"Yes, the funeral was yesterday, which was where I was given a letter from him instructing me to come here."

Hector felt extremely uncomfortable, not only because of meeting Barbara for the first time, but also due to the style of his surroundings, which could not have been further removed from his beloved Singapore.

"I guess what the first question is: How were you involved with Thomas?" It seemed to him that this was as good a point to start as any.

Barbara took a swig from her whisky, and, leaning forward with her hands cupping the whisky on her knees, she replied, "Involved? Don't make it sound sordid, morbid or illegal, my lad. If you had bothered to take a bit more of an interest in each other's lives, you'd have known that, for the past twenty-seven years, we've been what the younger ones call 'off 'n' on', and, if I'm honest, it was more on than off." She blushed, puffed on her cigarette, and finished her drink. Getting up, and pouring herself a refill, she continued. "Like most relationships, after the honeymoon period it went a bit sour for a while, but that was the only point at which it did so. After that, everything was roses all the way. Tommy used to stay here when he was in between the auctions, clearance sales and bargain hunts. He didn't have anywhere of his own really, and, from early on, this sort of became his home. As you can see, he adored Elvis."

Hector gazed around the room, picking out the clock on the wall, which had Elvis swinging his legs back and forth to keep time, and the miniature Elvis figurine on top of the television, which had been dressed in a Hawaiian-themed costume.

Barbara carried on talking. "He spoke of you often – his big brother in the East, the wealthy businessman with a nice home, expensive clothes, and hot and cold running servants. It sounds like he was jealous, but he wasn't. He was proud of you – so proud, in fact, that he never came out there to see you for the simple fact that he didn't consider that he was good enough. I told him until I was blue in the face that it wouldn't be like that, that you'd love to have him over and show him the sights. You would've, wouldn't you?"

"Goes without saying," said Hector. "By the way, what are those cigarettes? They're very bright."

Barbara pulled a packet out of her housecoat pocket. "Sobranie Cocktails. Expensive – but, then, for Christmas it's nice to be a bit different, isn't it? Try one?"

Hector picked a green-papered cigarette which had a gold-coloured filter, lit it with the aid of Elvis the lighter, sat back and almost began to relax a little.

At this point, Bonnie walked into the room and hopped into her armchair. She circled several times, and settled down on the knitted blanket, keeping one eye fixed on Hector. "She'll get used to you, don't worry," said Barbara. "She was Tommy's. Went everywhere together, they did. Good little guard dog for the van. A pug, snappy and yappy, aren't you, my darling?" The pug glanced at Barbara, and then carried on staring at Hector. "Best not to touch her just yet; she's got a nasty nip on her, even though she's getting on."

The pair went through what is known as a pregnant pause, slightly uneasy, and not sure of how far either could go with probing questions.

"How long are you around for then, before going back to Singapore?" Barbara said at last.

"I'm not altogether sure, really," Hector said, still keeping an eye on Bonnie, and taking a closer look at the Elvis figurine on the television. It had a small button which he pressed, and 'You Ain't Nothing but a Hound Dog' crackled out from somewhere under Elvis's loud shirt. Not amused, he sat down again and finished his drink.

"Another?" enquired Barbara. For what seemed like a short amount of time, or at least until Hector checked his watch and saw how much time had swept by, they shared stories about Thomas Barnes. It became more apparent that he had been what Barbara called 'a different kettle of fish' to the man sat in front of her now. It was hard to believe that they were brothers. She jumped to her feet and twittered, "It's almost twelve. Go on, I'll put the TV on. There's usually something from Big Ben on."

She poured good measures of whisky into each tumbler, flicked the television on, and together they sat on the sofa watching people dance around Trafalgar Square, waving at the cameras. The chimes of Big Ben announced the New Year, and a group of television celebrities sang 'Auld Lang Syne' in the studio.

As the screen filled with streamers and balloons, Barbara hoisted herself to her feet, left the room for a short while, and returned, saying, "I've fixed a bed up in one of the rooms for you. You'll be okay in there, and the bathroom is opposite you on the landing."

Hector took this to mean that, for the time being, this was the end of their discussion. Knocking back the last of his drink, he got up and followed Barbara up the stairs, where she carried on up the next flight to her bedroom.

She paused on the stairs, indicated his room with a pointed finger, and whispered loudly, "In there, Hector. It's not the Singapore Hilton, but it'll do for you. See you in the morning." With that, she was gone.

The house seemed still, and Hector discovered that, once undressed and in bed, his feet hung off the end. Every single movement brought a squeak from somewhere in the single divan, and, due to the New Year's Eve parties in the locality, people were starting to fight and throw up loudly outside in Argyll Road. He also found that, in a twisted comparison to Vicky's igloo of a spare room, this little bedroom was hotter than the inside of a toaster on full power; so, halfway through the night, he was kicking bed linen off himself and roasting quietly.

He got out of bed, went for a pee in the avocado-coloured loo on the landing, and, returning to the furnace of a bedroom, peeked out of the window. He gasped in shock at what appeared to be a stonemason's yard on the other side of the road. A drunken couple were in the middle of lovemaking, and clinging on to the statue of an angel who had the decency to look skywards rather than at what was going on at ground level. They were rocking to and fro in rhythmic flow, their breath clouding into the cold night like the plume from a steam train. Hector shook his head in disgust, groaned and sank back onto the bed, where eventually he fell asleep.

The first morning of a New Year arrived covered in frost. A couple of pigeons were pecking away at some kebab remains that were frozen to the pavement outside the newsagent's on the corner of Argyll Road, and the main road still had a few partygoers making their tortured way home after an all-nighter party, which had left them in a less than jaded state.

Barbara had decreed that the best way for Bonnie to get over her anxieties with Hector was for him to escort her on her morning walk. Therefore, the few stragglers in the High Street, that were clinging to a bus shelter for salvation, were treated to the sight of a middle-aged pug bouncing along the pavement with a tall gentleman following behind holding the lead as if it were highly contaminated by something nasty.

Hector bought a newspaper and took Bonnie down to the cliff top, where they stood for a while, both taking the fresh and crisp morning air. He found a bench and sat for a short while doing the crossword, while Bonnie amused herself nearby, seeking out strange and interesting smells and doing the things that a dog enjoys doing when out of the house.

They returned home about an hour later to find Barbara in the kitchen, emptying the contents of a frying pan onto two plates. Bonnie got her hopes up, only to have them dashed by Barbara telling her in no uncertain terms, "Oh no, my darling, not this. You know what happened the last time you had a bit of black pudding. Yours is over there, next to the washing machine, where it always is." Showing Bonnie that her bowl had been filled with food and biscuits, she motioned to Hector that their breakfast would be taken in the small dining room next to the living room, and not next to the washing machine with Bonnie.

Hector eyed the plateful of fried food that he knew was titled 'Full English Breakfast', yet it was swimming in so much fat that his arteries were crying out for exemption.

"It's not what I'm used to," said Hector, keen not to give offence. "At home in Singapore I usually settle for some green tea and Chinese sponge cake. Occasionally, if at a breakfast meeting, we have congee, which is the oriental breakfast – a bowl of rice starch and spring onions, similar to porridge, only with a raw egg cracked into it. Hardly ever do I see a breakfast like this, unless I'm in Australia or the United States. They do breakfast big time there."

Barbara placed her bacon and black pudding in between two pieces of toast, and squashing it together, took a mouthful. After a sip of tea, with her brow furrowed in a quizzical way, she asked, "A raw egg? Cracked into a bowl of Chinese porridge? That's certainly not my cup o' tea," and laughed loudly at her own joke. "Cup o' tea – get it? and not green tea either. What's that when it's at home?"

Hector stirred his tea. "It's extremely good for the digestion, and is wonderful for detoxing the system. I've sworn by it for years, but can't seem to find any here. I'd have thought the shops would have some by now, knowing how the world has gone crazy for health kicks and the body-beautiful ethos."

With that, he buttered some toast, piled the bacon, black pudding and tomatoes on top of it, and ate heartily, surprised at just how good it tasted.

'Not what I'd choose every morning, but that's probably why I enjoyed it,' he mused to himself. "I haven't had black pudding since I was a kid on holiday in Ireland with Thomas. We had a lovely time together, every summer holiday in Kerry, on the Dingle Peninsula. Do you know it?"

Clearing the empty plate with a smile on her face, Barbara said, "Black pudding was always one of Tommy's favourites. Now you've told me why. I can't say I know Ireland very well, although there was an item about it on the holiday programme on TV the other night that made it look very nice."

39

Chapter Three

You Can Choose Friends, But Not Family

A loud crash followed by the slamming of the front door startled both of them, and brought Bonnie barking into the hallway.

"It's me! I went, saw, and well and truly conquered. Now I'm home. Happy New Year, dear one. Any tea in the pot? I've got a mouth like a sumo wrestler's jockstrap."

Bonnie stopped barking, sneezed violently, and went into the living room, where she hopped onto her knitted throne and began licking her paws.

The origin of the noise and announcement made a whirling entrance into the dining room and stopped dead in his tracks. "Who are you? Did Barbara win a prize last night in the pub raffle?" Giggling, the tall, slim young man held out his hand to Hector. "Stuart's the name – by day anyway. Pleased to meet you."

Hector looked at him with disdain, and thought what a rude, gauche and florid young individual this was. He was almost certainly one of 'those' types of people, with whom he had absolutely nothing in common.

Barbara gushed into the dining room with a fresh pot of tea, wreathed in smiles. "Did you have a nice time, dear? How was London? This is Hector, Tommy's brother. He'll be with us for a few days, won't you, love? Hector, this is Stuart. He stays with me most of the time – out of season, at least. Have you just smashed a geranium pot in the porch on your way in?"

"It got in the way, or decided to commit suicide, I'm not sure which. Anyway, I'll buy you some bulbs or something, so you can plant fresh and bring the porch back to life for the start of the season."

Stuart draped himself around a dining chair, and sipped his tea with an air of refinement.

Hector got up, and, without a word or look towards Stuart, went into the kitchen and began wiping up the dishes that Barbara was washing in the sink.

"I'm amazed that you entertain his kind in this place," he said as he wiped plates with gusto. "Doesn't it put your guests off?"

Barbara stopped washing and laid a teacup back into the soapy water. "We don't have that sort of talk here, Hector, so get over yourself. You don't know anything about him, never mind what he's done for me since he came into my life. As a matter of fact, the guests love him. I'll agree that he can take some getting used to initially, but that's just who he is; and, under all the show, he's a lovely and decent young man. The sooner you understand that, the better it'll be for all of us." That said, she picked up the tea cup again and rubbed furiously at it, before handing it to him with a very final, "Okay?"

He realised he had overstepped the mark with her, but you couldn't change how he felt. It was his generation – their lack of tolerance for such individuals and the like. It didn't take rocket science to understand that his way of life and Stuart's were worlds apart. However, he knew that he had upset Barbara, and he really didn't want to do that, so making short work of the drying-up, and hanging the damp tea towel over the oven door handle, he turned and asked, "Do you have anything planned for today? I thought we could take a walk and find somewhere open, perhaps for lunch or something. Do you fancy that?"

Barbara could see in his face that he was trying, but she had no intention of letting him off that easily. "Sounds like a lovely idea. I'll ask Stuart if he would like to come with us, shall I?"

Not waiting for a reply, she went back to the dining room where Stuart was still draped over a chair, cup in hand, staring out of the window and daydreaming.

"I heard everything, dear one. You really shouldn't worry. His type will never alter its point of view, and I've come across many of them so often that I've got hardened to their Victorian mentalities. Ironic really, isn't it? As for joining you two for lunch, I'd love to, but I am totally knackered after last night. I think it's a case of beauty sleep for me now, so you won't mind if I leave him to you for the rest of the day. Ask him about Jakarta, or wherever it is that he lives. He's bound to go on about it for hours."

Stuart climbed the stairs with Bonnie close behind him, and went to his room for a long rest after what had been a hedonistic and energy-charged night out in London, first working, then partying away into the small hours before catching a ride home to Bournemouth with a couple of friends.

Bonnie, as Barbara told Hector whilst they were on their way out of the door, had always been particularly fond of Stuart, and whenever he was at home the little dog would not be far away from his side.

41

Making sure her headscarf was well tied, Barbara took Hector's arm and together they walked along the beach path that ran from Boscombe Pier all the way along to Bournemouth Pier. Once the day got under way, the temperature rose a few degrees and the frost disappeared. Although the wind coming in off the sea was littered with razor-sharp kisses, the weak winter sun managed to peep out from behind the clouds every so often, and both Hector and Barbara agreed that it was the best thing to wipe away the cobwebs.

They found a café near the town centre, once they had strolled through the well-manicured gardens. Despite it being the middle of winter, the climate had generally been kind to the south coast, and the gardens attracted many of the townsfolk walking off hangovers and enjoying the sea air. Consequently, the café was busy. Hector guided Barbara to a small table where they perched, and presently ordered tea and a toasted teacake each.

Once tea was poured and teacakes buttered, they sat enjoying the quiet, not feeling the need to converse solely for the sake of conversation.

Hector broke off a piece of teacake, popped it into his mouth and, taking a sip of tea, said, "There's something I've been meaning to ask you, Barbara. I hope you won't mind, but it's something that Thomas mentioned to me in his letter."

Barbara folded the butter wrapper over with her knife, and, pushing it to the side of her plate, took a deep breath. "I'm sure I can imagine what it is – after all, that's why you came to me in the first place, isn't it? Not for the delights of a second-rate guest house set back in a run-down side street, I'll bet!" She bit purposefully into her teacake, and took a moment to chew while she watched Hector growing more uncomfortable by the second in front of her. "It's the tea caddy, I know. He said I was to keep it until such time as you knocked on my door. I just didn't imagine you'd be here so soon after . . . " She swallowed hard and drank some tea. "You don't seem to have given much time and thought to the fact that I – we loved each other very much. Hand in glove, that's what he always said. Stuck here, running that place week in, week out, you don't get much time to get out and socialise. It was a special night when we first met all those years ago. I suppose you had been in the East for about eight to ten years by that stage – too wrapped up in sapphires and diamonds to give a thought to your brother."

Hector leaned forward, dabbing his mouth with a paper napkin. "Don't underestimate my intention. There were many times that I asked him to come out for a visit. It was he who chose not to. He'd disappear into the British landscape for weeks on end, before I'd get a card for my birthday or Christmas, and that would be it until such gatherings like the last one we met at – a wedding in London about a year and a half ago. That was when I realised we were totally different people, and, even though I continued to invite him, he never came."

Barbara sniffed. "Two different people? You couldn't have put it better yourself. Well, it's not just the tea caddy, Hector: there's something else Thomas left – a son! Now, can you guess who it is?"

Hector wiped his hands with the napkin. His palms were sweaty, and he could feel the colour rising in his cheeks.

Barbara was not going to be stopped, not even in a café in the middle of Bournemouth. "Yes – Stuart! My and Tommy's son. No matter how he grew up and turned out, we have loved him, and I will continue to do so." Barbara paused briefly, weighing up things. She decided that, since she was in full flow and by now had his undivided attention, as well as that of the two tables either side of her, she would carry on. "He's as hard as nails that boy. He's a drag queen, by the way."

The lady at the next table dropped her soup spoon, and Barbara slipped her a sideways glance laced with venom.

"He works very hard, travelling all over the place doing shows and making people happy. He's very good to me and loved his dad, who accepted him. They bonded beautifully. We had such a happy home when everyone was together. That's what kept me going when they were both away working. He's not daft either, Hector. It's already sinking into him that you are his uncle, so I'd advise you to start again with him. Let your blinkers and prejudice drop away for a change, and get to know the boy."

By this time, the soup on the next table had cultivated a skin on the surface and Hector felt that everyone was watching him, which wasn't altogether untrue. Barbara's voice had grown in volume as she had got more passionate, and this embarrassed him into an altogether different silence.

Hector paid the bill, and they left the café with an audience stuck to their chairs wondering if there would be more.

They got the bus back to Boscombe, and walked together down Argyll Road without a word spoken.

There was no sign of anyone at home, so Barbara noted to anyone who cared to listen that "Bonnie's gone for a walk with Stuart."

She went into the Elvis living room and, getting on her hands and knees, rustled around in a cupboard. She removed piles of LPs and stacks of antique-fair catalogues, until she was marooned on an island surrounded by mementos from the past.

After a small amount of cursing and teasing from the back of the cupboard, she pulled out the tea caddy. She stood up holding it triumphantly for Hector to view. He took the caddy from Barbara as if it were an unexploded bomb, and carried it across to the window, where he could admire it better in the light. The inlaid woodwork was of exceptional craftsmanship. It was plain to see that there had been many long hours of detailed work carried out, all in the effort to produce something that would hold tea. People forget that in the 18th century tea was a valuable commodity, treasured and sought after by the nobility at very high prices.

Since Thomas had been doing the antiques circuit for a number of years, it stood to reason that he would have a good eye for such things and be able to pick out top-quality items to hold onto for himself, for when a rainy day would dampen the finances.

Alas! that had not been the plan that fate had in mind, so it was Hector now holding the caddy, looking out of the window at the stone angels across the road, and wondering what he had done to deserve a ready-made instant set of relatives. Before coming to England, he had been alone in the world, except for Thomas, and now there was no Thomas, but a sort of sister-in-law, and a rather unique nephew who wore women's clothing for a living.

'My God!' he thought to himself. 'I've got to lie down and take this all in.'

Taking the caddy, Hector went upstairs to his room, leaving Barbara muttering to herself as she read the backs of some old LPs which Thomas had brought home from a car boot sale.

With the curtains pulled, and the daylight fading outside, Hector felt that he was lying in some kind of limbo. He had heard talk of the twilight zone, but, until now, had not had a real enough perception of it to base an opinion on. But, then again, thinking along the same lines, he had always been rigid and forthright with his thoughts and ideas. That had been the only way to conduct oneself in the colonies, and, moreover, the only way to start and run a profitable business. Naturally, from time to time, the company suffered small setbacks. The recent SARS epidemic had forced Singapore and its neighbours to make drastic cuts across their economies. Business had suffered, as had tourism. Consequently, Hector had dipped into one of his offshore nest eggs, and this had helped to rebalance the books, much to Jean's relief. All this, and the good way of life he had enjoyed for a number of years, was due to his principles in both business and social circles, and the high standard he had always set for himself. Such ideas, inspired by things like the twilight zone, and every other type of superstition, meant nothing to him. The good Lord and the Bible had made things clear enough, and, whilst he didn't attend services regularly, he felt that he had a cornerstone of the Christian faith to guide him. In such realms as these, there was definitely no room for queers. Here was the issue that perplexed Hector a great deal. Despite his orientation, Barbara had gone to great lengths to sing Stuart's praises, and, when all was said and done, it was plain to see that Thomas had loved his son, and even made a point of getting on with him.

'Can people really change so much?' Hector thought to himself as he heard Bonnie sniff and snort her way along the bottom of his closed door before she bobbed downstairs to investigate Jim Reeves, who could be heard having a quick session in the Elvis lounge. Barbara was doing the backing vocals while she refilled the cupboard.

Thomas had always been on the offensive when it came to sharing company with queers. Jokes, verbal and practical, had always been his penchant, so it was akin to throwing sweeties to a small child for Thomas to be presented with an openly homosexual and effeminate man. He relished every minute of making the individual's life hell on earth, and there were many stories that Hector could recall from their adolescent years. Now, it seemed, the Almighty had decided to test his servant, and had sent Thomas a queer for a son.

According to Barbara, the boy had bonded well with his father, and all had lived this hunky-dory life together.

'Well, there's nothing for it,' Hector decided as he sat up and pulled on a jumper. 'I'll give the boy a chance, and see what sort of a man he really is.' This seemed very matter of fact to him, yet it was dormant at the back of his mind that, for the solidity and future strength of family, something the Church was well in favour of, he would need to look towards Barbara and Stuart. What would Jean say? Would Alex say anything at all?

Hector sauntered downstairs and, putting the kettle on, prepared tea for three. He carried the tray into the lounge, where he was treated to the sight of mother and son howling their version of 'Stand by Your Man', before they collapsed onto a row of Elvis cushions and dissolved into giggles, tinged with a tear or two.

"There's nothing like a good sing-song to make things feel right again," said Stuart, as he accepted a mug of tea from Hector.

Barbara was slightly flushed, but, after wiping her eyes with her handkerchief and hiding it away back up her sleeve, she blew on the hot tea, and glanced at the men either side of her as she sipped.

"I'd hate to think we had got off on the wrong foot with each other," Hector said calmly. "Since your mother has informed me of the background history which has accompanied recent events, it is perhaps time for us to get to know each other a bit more."

45

Stuart looked at Hector without giving away anything. He simply folded his arms, and rested his chin in the palm of his hand. 'It's important to Mum for me to listen now to what this old fossil had to say. So let's give him a go,' thought Stuart, with a slight curl of a smile on his face as Hector continued.

"If both of you hold passports, I'd like you both to come back to Singapore with me, and let me give you a short holiday there. Since Thomas never came, it seems only right that you two should make the journey. What do you think?"

It appeared to him that Stuart and Barbara were struck dumb for a minute as they sat on the Elvis sofa taking his proposition into account.

"Well, we've both got passports. We went to Spain for a week last autumn," Barbara said at last, looking to Stuart for backup, and hoping for some input from him.

Stuart got up and poured himself a whisky, went to the kitchen, filled up the tumbler with cola, and returned to the living room, having been watched the whole time by Hector and his mother as if they were spectators at a tennis match. Bonnie had trotted to the kitchen and back, disappointed not to have heard a biscuit tin being opened.

Stuart had a swig of his drink, lit a cigarette, and sat back on the sofa. "It's a good idea. We should go, Mum. I'm sure Hector here has lots to show us. After all, it must be a totally different way of life from this gem by the sea. But, before we go, there's a condition. Hector, you have to spend another fortnight with us and meet some of Dad's friends. That's the only way you'll get to know the type of person he really was, and also you need to come and see one of my shows. Not only are they so completely marvellous, but it'll loosen your colonial corset for you, and that won't hurt for one night, will it?" He took another sip, and smiled sweetly at Hector.

Barbara stood up, saying, "That's it, then – two weeks here with us, and then two weeks there with you. Fish fingers for tea – all right?"

Stuart went out for the evening to meet friends for drinks, and Barbara emerged from her room nursing a shoebox stuffed with photos and memorabilia, which she and Hector sifted through while Bonnie sat on her blanket and watched. As they looked at old pictures, it dawned on Barbara that, although he had the life of Riley, Hector didn't have any family or close friends, so it was doubtful whether he would have a shoebox of memories like this at home in Singapore. She could see, each time his face lit up and smiled at a picture of Thomas, that he now realised what he had missed out on, so she was adamant that the time they would have for the next couple of weeks would not be wasted.

"That's Horace," she said, pointing to a large square man in a picture, stood next to Thomas at the back of a van, with its doors open and a young Bonnie poking her head round to see what was going on. "For a while, he and Tommy were partners; but it didn't really work, so they ended up doing their separate things. But they remained friends, which I think is quite something in this day and age. Did you see him at the funeral?"

"There were a lot of people like him there," said Hector as he accepted a magenta-coloured cigarette. "To be honest, they all kind of looked the same, and, besides, I don't think I was in the right frame of mind, anyway."

"No, you wouldn't have been. We'll have to seek out Horace and take him to lunch. The last time I heard, he was in Salisbury, and I know where he likes to hang out, so we're bound to find him."

For a few days, things returned to their routine normality. Barbara cleaned the house from top to bottom as 'it wouldn't do itself', and Stuart either slept a lot or played CDs loudly in his room.

"Rehearsing," said Barbara in a hushed voice filled with excited reverence.

Hector and Bonnie took their walks in the mornings and afternoons, even discovering at last, in one of the small general stores, a packet of green tea. This was borne home with great relief and triumph, only for Hector's hopes to be dashed by both Barbara and Stuart's expressions as they gingerly sipped the brew.

"That's awful – and no milk or sugar either! No, I couldn't get used to that," Barbara said.

"Obviously an acquired taste – perhaps it tastes better in an oriental environment," scoffed Stuart.

Despite being slightly crestfallen, Hector accepted the fact that it wasn't to everyone's liking, rather like so many things these days. Nevertheless he sat comfortably in the living room reading the local newspaper, sipping his green tea, with Bonnie flaked out at his feet in front of the three-bar electric fire.

One afternoon, Hector met Bob and Vicky for tea and cakes in Bournemouth. Vicky was all over Bonnie like a rash, fussing and gushing. Bob listened as Hector told them what had transpired since they had parted on New Year's Eve.

"Quite a roller coaster for you, then, with one thing and another," Bob said, cutting his eclair. "You have to accept the facts that, firstly, Thomas really did leave you something more than a mere token and joke, and that, consequently, you have to refocus your ideas, and even your lifestyle to make room for those two. By the way, have you spoken to Jean? She called us the other morning, so I just said you had gone away for a few days, and that you'd be in touch. If you haven't already, I suggest you give her a tinkle."

Hector blushed with guilt, and made a note to call the office.

"There's no need to blush, dear," said Vicky between mouthfuls of gateau. "Almost everyone these days knows someone gay. There's nothing wrong with them, and it's not like they've just landed on the planet. They've been around for hundreds of years. Even when I was younger, the girls and I always had a gay friend with whom we could have laughs, cry our eyes out, and get good advice and the most amazing guidance on what to wear to impress our boyfriends."

For the first time, Hector mused as to what Stuart would say if he were confronted with Vicky, and, stopping himself from laughing out loud, he changed the subject. "How's Bernie? It was so nice to meet her at Christmas."

"Oh, she's fine – still swearing at kids, and doing the yoga classes with Vicky, isn't she?" said Bob as he watched her cram another mini mountain of cake into her mouth. "Since they both agreed that they overdid it on the calorie scale at Christmas, they're talking about doing the Atkins diet – aren't you, love?" and Bob smiled to himself as he eyed Hector over the rim of his teacup.

"Well, it's all a question of timing – when to start and all that. Today is not the day, that's for certain. Would the little doggie like some cake?" Vicky said as she scooped a smudge of cream onto her little finger.

Bonnie, who had been quietly minding her business under the table, ventured out for the treat, and licked Vicky's finger clean.

Having sat up late watching a film on the television, Hector checked his watch for the time difference and phoned Jean.

Briefly going over what had happened to him since Christmas Day, he asked if all was well in Singapore.

"Nothing we can't handle without you," Jean said efficiently but kindly. "So, when are you coming home? I'll need to book two extra seats for your travelling companions, won't I? Raffles class or economy?"

Hector thought for a moment, his gaze fixed on the bald spot in the hallway carpet. "Make it Raffles for them too, please, Jean. They could do with being spoilt a bit. I'm here for another week or so, so make the reservations for the night flight on the 17th. That should be enough. That way, they've got time to get ready, and you've got time to set out my working diary for the rest of the month. There must be a backlog building up."

He could hear Jean sigh. "As I keep telling you, everything is fine."

Of course, having a date to work around makes my life a tad easier. I'll get on to the jewellery designers for that meeting, and the people in Sydney wanted to fly up to talk opals. Alex has just gone by. He said to say hello. I'll make sure he's at Changi to meet you all. You can collect the other tickets at Heathrow when you fly out."

Hector loved it when Jean talked like this – all organised and accounted for. It relaxed any tensions in his mind, and reassured him that things would be as she said, for they wouldn't dare to be otherwise. "Thank you, Jean. You're a – well, you know."

"Yes, I know. Now go off and get to know Barbara and Stuart a bit more, will you? – after all, they're what Thomas has left you, and are worth more than a tea caddy."

Hector slept well that night. It had been good to talk to Jean, and only now did he realise that he actually missed her – more so, in fact, than he would otherwise have thought.

The following morning, he found both Barbara and Stuart waiting for him in the kitchen.

"We're going out for the day to find Horace for lunch in Salisbury." Stuart sounded quite excited. "We haven't seen him for absolutely ages, and there's nothing quite like a good Horace hunt!"

Barbara rustled around in her handbag, producing a bag of boiled sweets. "I've got these for the journey, and Stuart's borrowed a car from one of his friends for the day, so we don't have to muck about with the trains," she said excitedly.

They piled into the 4-door saloon car and, with Bonnie planted on Hector's lap in the back seat, they set off for Salisbury, arriving there just before the lunch hour.

Having parked near the cathedral, and having admired the spire, which is known to be the tallest in England, they walked to a pub with low beams and a decidedly Elizabethan feel to it.

Barbara led the way as they entered the bar. "He'll be in here, I'm sure of it. It's his regular lunchtime haunt."

Sure enough, she squealed with delight, threw her arms wide, and flew across the floor to where a man was sat on a bar stool just finishing a pint of Guinness.

The vision of Barbara swooping down on him gave Horace a bit of a shock. "Well, what you doin' 'ere, me darlin'?" he growled as he squeezed her, almost making her disappear in his broad-shouldered bear hug.

"Oh! It's a long story, love, but let me introduce you. This is Hector – Tommy's brother from Singapore. Stuart – well, you know him already!"

Horace sucked his teeth, and teased a piece of trapped breakfast

49

from the side of his mouth with his tongue. "So, he's dead, then."

It seemed to Hector that everyone only expected to be introduced to him on the assumption that his brother was deceased. He felt more like the Grim Reaper each time it happened. "Yes, I'm afraid so. But Barbara's been wonderful, and said we should come and look you up. Another Guinness?"

Horace never turned down the offer of a Guinness, and, while Hector got drinks at the bar, he moved from his bar stool across to a table and chairs which were strategically placed near a crackling fireplace. Together, everyone sat relating old stories about Thomas.

They had lunch, and left the pub around two thirty.

"Can we give you a lift anywhere?" offered Stuart as he unlocked the car.

"Wouldn't mind," accepted Horace as he launched himself into the back seat of the car. "Back to my shop, if that's okay. I'll show you the way. You haven't seen it, have you?"

Barbara talked over her shoulder as they drove through the town. "You? With a shop? Gosh, you're all organised suddenly. What prompted the change?"

Horace held on to the car door as they coasted round a traffic roundabout, Stuart driving, and imagining himself as Anna being waltzed round a ballroom in *The King and I*.

"I just got tired of waiting in the rain for sales and auctions. Now, they come to me in my shop, and I've built up quite a good stock. Left here, Stewy, then second right. It's on the left-hand side, about halfway down."

Although Stuart disliked anyone shortening his name, especially to Stu, he made an exception in Horace's case. He was very fond of the old thing, and had known him since his father had taken him to an auction where he had been introduced as 'the nipper'. Anything was an improvement on this, as nipper sounded more like a retired racing greyhound to Stuart than a term of endearment for a small child. However, you couldn't change folks like Horace, or for that matter, he guessed, Hector too.

They arrived at Horace's shop, and, at his insistence, all went in for a look round. It was jam-packed with items purchased over the years. There were two glass display cases which held antique jewellery. Hector stood rooted to the spot, looking at the array of rings, brooches and bracelets on show. Stuart was inspecting a heavy brass deep-sea diver's helmet, and Barbara was stood in between the outstretched paws of a stuffed grizzly bear, which kept counsel at the back of the shop.

It seemed as if everyone was saying, "Look at this," at the same time, thereby letting Horace know he had a good thing going as he returned from his small office behind a heavy velvet curtain, clutching a box tied together with string.

"I guess you'll have seen one of these before," he said to Hector as he pulled a tea caddy out of the box.

"But it's identical to the one that Barbara gave me," said Hector as he took a closer look at the tea caddy. "Do you mean to tell me that they mass-produced these things?"

"Not quite, but in this case there were a pair made by specific commission from a local lord." Horace opened a drawer nearby and pulled out a faded document. "This is the request and bill from the maker. It's always good to have documents as proof that these things are genuine. You can take this – it's good for your tea caddy, and may help increase the value should you decide to sell it."

Hector looked horrified. "Sell it? I couldn't do that, ever, but the papers are interesting to have, so I wouldn't mind having them, if that's okay by you."

"'S'fine by me," said Horace who couldn't care less. "It'll be fun to know that I've got mine here, and you've got yours all the way over there in Singapore."

Stuart noticed the time and mentioned that they should be leaving. "We've got to get back. I'm doing a show tonight, so I need time to get ready. You know how it is."

Horace could only wonder, but, giving Barbara another bear hug of a squeeze, had her promise to return soon.

They got in the car, after walking Bonnie up and down the road several times. "Just to make sure she doesn't go all over your leg," shrieked Barbara, and they drove back to Boscombe in time for a light meal, before heading off with Stuart to his show.

Hector hadn't planned on going, but, after a nice day together, he didn't want to upset the harmony that had developed. So, with Gloria Gaynor blaring out of the car stereo, they set off for an evening of cabaret, care of Stuart Barnes, appearing tonight as Tinkie la Trash. Hector could only hazard a guess at what he was about to witness.

The J & J Club had been established in the mid-eighties, and since then had maintained a fairly high profile on the south coast gay scene. As is so often the case, due to the licences that the club held for late hours and cabaret shows, it created a reputation for itself as not only somewhere to go for a drink when all the pubs had closed for the night, but also somewhere for good live entertainment. Coupled with the magic worked by the DJ in his music box, this meant that all sorts of people enjoyed an extended night out, thanks to J & J. These are not the initials of the club's owners, nor their matching Maltese poodles, but, as anyone will tell you, as if you were supposed to have known already, J & J stands for 'Joan and Joan', otherwise titled as Crawford and Collins.

It was the Andy Warhol treated pictures of these two icons that looked at Hector as he followed Barbara and Stuart into what was already beginning to be a busy night for the venue.

"I love it like this. It means that the show will go well. They can't fail to adore me," purred Stuart as he swayed through the crowd at the bar and into a small but well-lit dressing room, which was squashed in between the stage and a toilet.

Barbara began unzipping suit carriers, revealing sequined long dresses with over-the-top designs on them, and Stuart laid out a selection of make-up on the table in front of the mirror that would have put Estée Lauder to shame.

Pulling a large and teased wig out of a box, Stuart crowed, "*Et voila!*"

Hector, who had been stood in the corner next to a small hand basin, jumped, and started to take stock of his surroundings. The Tiffin room at his beloved Raffles Hotel this was not, and having to consider himself as merely uncomfortable would have been an understatement.

"I wouldn't stand too close to the basin," said Stuart. "The gorgeous male strippers I sometimes work with usually use that for a piss, and the toilet's too far and too busy for them." Picking up a pint glass of stale lager, he added, "Although sometimes the basin's too much for them as well."

Pouring the lager down the basin's furry plughole, it dawned on Hector that this wasn't lager at all, and he knew this to be the perfect moment to leave and get a drink.

"Will they serve drinks to us?" he asked Barbara quietly.

"No, love. It's time to get out there and get a feel of the place. Don't worry, I'll come with you. The bar staff all know me, so we won't have to wait long to be served."

With that, she pecked Stuart on the cheek and ushered Hector out of the dressing room, pushing him towards the bar. They crossed the dance floor, which was filled with a mixed crowd of people. Hector noticed that, despite it being a pop song that he had never heard before, everyone seemed to know the particular dance steps to the tune, and subsequently were giving a star performance of their massed formation-dance-team routine.

The barman leaned across the bar and gave Barbara a warm hug and kiss. "This is Dale. He's from Australia, and pours a pretty mean mai tai. Dale, this is Hector. He would probably choose a Singapore sling, but tonight I think one of your delicious mai tai's is in order."

Dale beamed, said hello to Hector, and prepared the cocktails.

"It's very loud in here, isn't it?" said Hector. "I can hardy hear myself think."

Barbara passed him a cocktail, and taking a large suck through her straw nodded towards the crowd on the dance floor, and the DJ who was mixing in a new song. "It has to be. That's all part of the place's vibe. They've had the DJ for a while now, and he gets them all warmed up for the show." Waving at the DJ, she pointed at Hector and then at herself. "I told them we would be bringing you down," smiled Barbara.

Just then the DJ announced over the PA system that, "Tinkie's folks are in the J & J for the night."

Everyone cheered, and Hector wished that Jean were somewhere nearby. She'd know what to do. She had said, what seemed a long time ago, that he should enjoy himself. This hadn't been exactly what he had imagined – far from it – but he had to admit to himself that the beat was catchy, and how Stuart was going to hold this crowd's attention would have to be seen to be believed.

A fanfare and intro played over the speakers, and the dance floor filled with people, who, on the advice of the DJ, had topped up their drinks, and were now chattering away like a tree full of starlings at sunset.

After the intro, and on cue from a thumbs-up that stuck itself out of the dressing-room door, the crowd all hushed suddenly, only to have the silence split like an axe into a tree as Tinkie la Trash sprang onto the stage and began singing 'Que Sera Sera' aided by a backing track controlled from the DJ box. The audience joined in the chorus, and were all swinging from side to side in unison to the rhythm.

Even by the bar, Hector felt Barbara's arm curl round his waist and motion him from side to side. He downed the cocktail, and beckoned Dale over to make refills.

Half an hour later, and Tinkie had sworn, cursed, dealt mercilessly with hecklers, sung three more songs from the movies, and survived a finale of 'My Heart Will Go On' accompanied by three champagne bucketfuls of ice cubes, which had been launched by some of the crowd from the dance floor.

"That was the audience participation bit," Barbara hiccuped. "They love chucking ice cubes at her when the ship goes down. 'Iceberg Ahead' always gets them going."

Hector had to agree, and admitted that, despite his reservations, he had found the whole experience uplifting.

"That's what it's all about, though," Barbara said as she fished for a cherry in the bottom of her glass. "There's no barriers in this place. Everyone gets treated equally – no prejudice. I mean, God knows it's hard enough in the real world for some of these folks. A bit of escapism never hurt anyone once in a while."

"The mai tai helped a bit too," laughed Hector, "but I think it was more than a couple that we've had. Where's Stuart?"

The music had started up again, and, feeling the heavy bass beat humming in his chest, Hector sailed off his bar stool and staggered to the dressing room.

Stuart had just finished removing his costume and make-up, his face shining with baby oil. "It gets everything off in double-quick time – an old trick, but it ruins the towels. Pick that up, would you? and we'll get out of here."

With that, he hopped into some flared jeans, pulled a tee shirt over his head, and sprayed some deodorant over his body. Clapping his hands and clicking his fingers at the same time, he gave an air of satisfied achievement, and indicated to Hector that they should move. He opened the door and led the way through a crowd, who voiced their appreciation loudly, back to where Barbara was now saying goodbye to Dale.

Hector felt rather conspicuous holding a polystyrene head with Stuart's wig planted on it, but he managed to shake it at the DJ as if he were a Tudor executioner, and, bowing slightly to the two Joans, thanked the large but polite lesbian bouncer, and stumbled out into the cold night air looking for the car.

"C'mon, Tinks, time to go home and get your head down." Hector roared with laughter at his own joke.

"How many mai tais did Dale give you guys?" said Stuart as he drove them home.

"Dunno, darlin', but it did him some good – at last," replied Barbara as she pulled off her clip-on earrings, which were pinching her to distraction.

Between the two of them, they managed to carry Hector up to his room, and, after a lot of protesting, left him to sleep with Tinkie's head next to him on the pillow.

"It must have been hitting the cold air that got those mai tais whizzing around in him. I'm surprised he didn't chuck up," said Stuart as he made coffee in the kitchen, and fussed over Bonnie, who was delighted at their return.

"I think we can count that as one to us," smirked Barbara. "I'd like to see what Singapore can come up with to match that for a night out."

54

Each carrying a mug of coffee, they retired to their rooms, kissing goodnight to each other on the landing.

Barbara rubbed her ear lobes, and applied more night cream than required to her arms and neck, whilst Stuart let Bonnie scuttle through his legs and hop onto his bed. Closing his bedroom door, he exhaled emphatically as if to underline the relief of having had his uncle see his show.

The following day, Hector had the curse of a mai tais hangover, which is something not to be wished on anyone, and he spent most of the morning curled up in his bed. Each tiny movement seemed to scream pain around his body. Had it been worth it, though? Well, Stuart could sing, there was no doubt about that. His command of the crowd was a mix of regimental and pantomime, which seemed to work extremely well.

Stuart had said that not every crowd was a good one, and before now he had survived some bad nights and shows, not helped by having to change into Tinkie in cellars, the smallest of toilets, or even, on one occasion, the rusting shell of a small caravan which was next to a skip in a pub car park. "Heigh-ho!" he had said, "that's show business." The optimism sprang out of Stuart like Peter Pan's shadow on a play run. With nothing to dampen this bright light and quest for fame, he had been doing the circuit for a while, and it had been apparent to Hector from sitting at the bar in J & J's that people liked the act.

Some people had approached Barbara during the course of the night, telling jokes, being very familiar with her, their arms around her shoulders, quietly swapping secrets. He had also noticed several other women sat around the bar, all fairly similar in age and style to Barbara. "That'll be the Mum Squad," Dale had informed him. "They come in from time to time, have fun with their boys, and then go home. A couple of them come with their gay sons, and one with her lesbian daughter. One comes on her own, who lost her son last year. Coming here makes her feel close to him. Time for a mai tai?"

Hector lay quite still, replaying the previous night in his mind's eye, catching as many pictures as he could. Peter Pan's shadow? An interesting comparison really, as there were a lot of people in the club who seemed to be holding on to their youthful spirits as long as they could, giving a strong rebuff to the onslaught of old age. Of course, old age to people like that meant anything above fifty, so Hector had felt like a dinosaur on the bar stool. Was he that much out of touch?

Barbara crept into the room with some aspirins, water, and a plastic bucket, which she put by the bed. "Just in case, dear. Come on down when you feel up to it."

Hector wondered for a moment if he would ever feel up to it again. Eventually, though, he managed to come downstairs to the living room, where Stuart gave him an egg sandwich, a bottle of fizzy water and a cup of green tea.

"You remembered!" croaked Hector gratefully.

"After the many times you mentioned it, we couldn't forget it. And since you said how good it was for getting rid of things, I thought it best for now, and there's an old film on the TV in a minute. They're always good to help get over hangovers. Now then, eat your sandwich."

Over the next couple of days, Barbara made several phone calls to some of the antiques crowd that Thomas had hung around with over the years. Subsequently, an evening get-together was arranged, and the Bide-a-Wee had more visitors in it than it had seen for quite a while.

Despite feeling awkward and clumsy, Hector soon found that the exchange of stories and laughter relaxed him, and he heard more about Thomas, which, as Barbara pointed out whilst shaking a tray of ice cubes into the plastic pineapple, "Can only help you to get a better picture of him, and help you to know that there were a lot of folk who got on with him, and who really liked his company. Nobody could spin a yarn like Tommy once he got going."

Hector remembered the wedding again, where he had last seen Thomas, and the image of him at the bar with all the menfolk of the bride's family around him made him smile to himself. At least now he could relate to what this group of friends were all talking about. Everyone greeted Stuart as if he were one of the gang. Still, they had all known him since he had been very young, going to antique fairs with his father. Over the years, some had spoilt him with small gifts and ice creams, and, later on, a nip of brandy from a hip flask on a cold morning.

Hector pondered, for the first time, on the thought that it may have been a great shame to live so far away, and miss out on all this; but, at the end of the day, he had his own life to live, business to run and, as some would no doubt say, empire to build. The price of all this was, of course, a kind of self-imposed social celibacy. He had forgotten when it stopped being such an issue, and the buying and selling of precious gems took over, becoming his own little family of sapphire sons, diamond daughters and ruby cousins.

"What price happiness?" someone said, and Hector jumped slightly, coming back into the foray of storytelling that was going on.

Everyone looked to him for some input, so, with a prompt from Stuart along the lines of 'Tell us what he was like as a kid,' he regaled the group with tales from years ago – snowball fights in winter, and long summer-afternoon adventure walks in the Irish countryside.

Everybody laughed at the practical jokes, which they all related to, and Hector warmed to the idea that here he felt included, and would not have to suffer the embarrassment of having someone approaching him with the words, "Your brother's dead, then?"

One morning, Hector returned with Bonnie after their walk together, to find Stuart in the hallway just replacing the telephone receiver.

"Well, that's a bit of luck," he smiled. "Gloria Gold's been taken into hospital with a kidney stone, so the agent's just asked me to fill in and do a show tonight with the boys. Now then, Hector, this you need to see – but no mai tai overdoses, okay?"

Hector let Bonnie off her lead, allowing her to go bouncing off towards the sound of Barbara's singing that was coming from the kitchen.

"A show? Not at that club again, is it?" he asked with a crease growing across his brow.

"Oh, no," said Stuart, the smile broadening into a big grin. "This venue's much more up your street. It's a British Legion Club in Southampton."

Hector squared himself up. "Oh, that sounds rather good. Yes, I'll come. Shall we be taking your mother?"

Stuart folded his arms. "I don't think so. She doesn't usually come with me for work. The J & J is different, and, besides, she lets herself go a bit there. This is real work. The agent will be there, and if they like what I do – and, more importantly, get a good reaction from the crowd – then I'll get more bookings in, which is good for this time of year. It's usually dead quiet in January."

Having established that the club had all its own sound equipment and minidisc players, which surprised both of them, Hector and Stuart set off with a heavy bag each and a couple of suit carriers. Not being so far away, there was no need for a car, so they took a train.

After a short journey by taxi from Southampton Central, at eight o'clock that evening, they arrived at the Royal British Legion Club. A steward met them and guided them through a smoke-filled bar where men were playing darts.

"Blimey!" shouted someone from a crowded table of domino players, "The stripper's gettin' on a bit, ain't he?" and nearly the whole bar blasted the air with mocking laughter.

"What do they mean, stripper?" enquired Hector as they entered a narrow, long room, designated for the evening as a changing room.

"Didn't I say?" said Stuart innocently. "It's a ladies' night in the function suite. Drag artiste, *moi*, and two strippers, the boys."

"Oh, my God!" mumbled Hector under his breath. "I thought that when you said the boys, you meant singers or something."

Stuart started emptying make-up and brushes, thick false lashes and lipstick onto a small table. "God, no! This is far more fun. The girls will go wild, and the boys are lovely – in character I mean, not just looks. You're going to be fine. Now go and get us a drink while I fight with these tights."

He found the bar in the function suite, and was served promptly by a pair of barmaids, who were looking forward to the night ahead.

Planting two drinks on the bar, one said, "So, you're with Tinkie, are you? We've been told he's good. Mind you, everyone's looking forward to the strippers. Sheila's brought her mum out for the night. At ninety-two she doesn't get out much, but wasn't going to miss this for the world, was she, Sheila?"

Sheila returned with change, and gave it to Hector, giggling, "Too bloody right. We've had our hair done especially for it, and it's been ages since Mum's seen a decent bit of man. So tonight she's going to cop the lot."

Hector choked on his sip, and, coughing, turned round to see a small elderly lady sat at a table surrounded by women of all ages. The suite was filling up quickly, so Hector took the drinks back to where Stuart had all but finished transforming himself into Tinkie and was in mid-conversation with a tall, handsome, and very muscular man, who Hector correctly assumed was one of the strippers.

"Meet Steve. He's on first tonight, though really he's so good he should be a finale, not an intro," he mewed.

It had decided itself really, but, whilst in his get-up, Hector could only think of Stuart as Tinkie. He preferred without a doubt, though, the Stuart at home, rather than this vision glittering in sequins before him. He shook hands with Steve, and discovered that the stripper had a sweet wife at home, to whom he'd been devoted for some time, and a young daughter, who was now and for ever the apple of his eye.

Steve and Tinkie discussed the various acts with which they had each shared an evening's work lately, and the general state of play on the circuit.

Listening on a small stool in the corner, Hector was amazed that people in the business settled for the comparatively small amount of money offered by agents, for performances they made at venues so far away from home.

On top of this, as Steve pointed out, despite being encouraged to accept the booking on the promise that a full house of sex-mad and booze-fuelled girls would buy all the promotion goodies that the strippers all sold, when eventually reaching a venue the stripper would discover that the audience totalled less than twenty, and that they had all brought their own cameras, making the need for glossy posters and souvenirs melt away as fast as the ice in their drinks. "Still, the show goes on, and we get to work with some good people like Tinks here," Steve concluded, grabbing him round the waist.

"Go and get yourself ready, babe. You're on in twenty," commanded Tinkie. Adjusting his false bosom, he marched out of the dressing room in seven-inch high heels, winking at Hector as he swept by, and out onto the stage, where the packed function suite erupted with cheers, whistles, and loud fairground-style laughter.

Twenty or so minutes later, and with the loud and heavy bass beat of the stripper's music intro making the dressing room vibrate, Tinkie stood in the doorway and leaned against the door. "Blimey, they're a wild bunch tonight, and dirty too. Still, it makes it easier to insult them all really." Lighting a cigarette, he added, "Are you okay for drinks? I need something – a brandy and lemonade perhaps – and NOW!" With that, he disappeared towards the bar, throwing insults at the lads playing pool as if they were meat titbits being cast into a pit full of starving hounds.

Hector sat listening to the reaction that the stripper was drawing from the excited crowd of women. Some life! and what a way to earn a living this must be! But, if that's what paid the bills and put food on the table, it wasn't his place to judge.

Tinkie returned triumphantly with drinks, and they had a couple of minutes for a smoke, change of gown, and a touch-up of the make-up before going back on stage. He thanked the stripper for coming, and launched into the second half of the show.

By now, a second stripper had arrived – apparently the finale act – and Steve had introduced the dazed young man, who had been slightly stunned to find Hector sat on a stumpy stool in a corner of the dressing room nursing a whisky. This young tease, for there was no more apt word for him, went by the name of Calvin. He was dressed in the most expensive and up-to-the-minute fashion gear, and rather fancied himself stood indoors with his sunglasses on.

Hector thought this was more like the classic image of a male stripper. Nothing against Steve, but, apart from the muscular body, he was altogether too safe and decent a soul to be around. He didn't smoulder like Calvin did. When you saw pictures of little men in red tights running around the hottest corners of hell with a toasting fork primed for your sorry and repenting soul, it was Calvin's naughty face that matched, and completed the picture.

Hector considered this as Calvin changed into a soldier's costume, and, with all his tools and tricks wrapped up in an English flag, he stomped off towards the approaching intro that Tinkie was having no problem whatsoever in warming the women up for.

It seemed rather a pity to Hector that, for such hard-working folk as these, who sometimes did two shows a night, there were such meagre facilities in which to get ready. The dressing room here was narrow, but at least well lit according to Tinkie, which made a change from a freezing-cold cubicle in the men's loo.

Tinkie finished the show with a number that got the whole audience on their feet and joining in.

To rapturous applause, and screams for another look at the strippers, he marched back into the dressing room, kicked off the high-heel shoes, and, leaning on the edge of the small hand basin, began to massage his feet."My God! that's enough for one night. Come on, Hector, be a dear and start packing up the stuff. We'll make the train at twenty to, rather than quarter past, if we get a move on."

Taking a large squirt of baby oil, he rubbed his face until the make-up came off and began to run down his neck, whereupon a towel was brought into action.

Shortly after, Hector said, "Welcome back, Stuart."

Stuart replied, "Hello, dear," with a wry smile.

It was while they were squashing make-up bags, towels and shoes into a bag that Steve poked his head around the door of the dressing room. "You're not going on the train, are you? I'm going to Poole now, and picking up the wife, who's been with her folks for the day. So, if you're ready now, I can drop you off in Boscombe."

Stuart was not going to turn down such an offer, so, with Hector folded up in the back seat of Steve's car, along with bags, costumes, and the already familiar wig, they drove out of Southampton and through the New Forest; getting back to Argyll Road just after midnight.

After thanking Steve, who had climbed out of the car in order to give Stuart a big muscle-bound bear hug, and who reconfirmed to Hector that Stuart was "One of the best in the business, and a good pal when the chips are down," uncle and nephew both dropped the bags in the hall, boiled the kettle for coffee, and discussed the evening's events.

Hector found that, despite having had biased ideas about the type of entertainment field that Stuart and, for that matter, Steve and Calvin too were involved in, he had to confess that his eyes had been opened.

Stuart, it was becoming apparent to him, was capable of delivering a good story at any time, based on his previous experiences as Tinkie, but Hector made it clear to him that it was as Stuart that he preferred him, and not the acid-mouthed drag queen, no matter how entertaining the show might be.

Listening, Stuart found that whereas before he had thought of Hector as a pompous old oaf, a fossil of bygone times, he now looked at his uncle in a slightly different way. It wouldn't be everyone, after all, who would have accompanied him to the show tonight, or the other night at the J.& J either – mai tai or not.

Bonnie yawned, gave a brief wag of her tail, and went upstairs to Stuart's room. It wasn't long before both Hector and Stuart followed her. Lying in bed, Hector wondered what Stuart would make of Singapore, or, for that matter, what on earth would Singapore think of Stuart?

Chapter Four

A Discovery in the Country

Although January is not considered the best month of the year in England for going to the countryside for a picnic, Barbara had other ideas. While Hector and Stuart were taking their time over breakfast one morning, she was wrapping food in foil, putting sandwiches in freezer bags and picking some fruit out of a bowl on the window sill.

"Right then, you two, let's get a bit livelier, shall we?"

This was met with blank stares from both men, so with a deep sigh she enlightened them with her plan for the day.

"I've decided we're going out to the countryside for the day. It's not too bad out there," she said, squinting through the net curtains. "At least it's dry anyway. Considering we're off to Singapore in a few days' time, Hector hasn't seen hardly anything of the area, so it's a case of making the most of the time we've got. Dale's lent us the car, and dropped it off outside earlier this morning while you two were still in bed. Bless him, I've always had a soft spot for Australians."

So had Stuart, who thought it better to keep the notion to himself.

"I spoke to Horace too, and he's going to meet up with us and have lunch. That'll be nice, won't it?" She looked for some reaction, which was beginning to emerge from the fog of Hector's early morning mind.

"Well, so long as it's not too cold, I think it'll be fun. Picnics aren't something that we do a lot of in Singapore – not in the British sense, anyway." Looking at Stuart across the table, he added, "I hope you're going to be able to accompany us too."

"He hasn't a choice in the matter," snapped Barbara emphatically. "We'll even take Bonnie for a change. She'll enjoy a day out. I'm sure Stuart can cope for at least one day without any work with Tinkie, can't you, dear?"

Stuart stubbed out a cigarette, and, looking at Bonnie, who had taken leave of her senses at the mention of her name, said softly, "I reckon we can manage that, don't you, Bon-Bon?"

Bonnie agreed wholeheartedly, and ran excitedly backwards and forwards between the kitchen and front door, unsure of where she was required to be, but at the same time keen not to be left behind.

After no more than the usual amount of fuss which preludes a British family outing, during which tartan blankets were traced and added to the already loaded provisions in the car, they set off. Stuart drove, Barbara gave directions and Hector did his utmost to control Bonnie's excitement in the back seat of the car.

The county of Dorset is often referred to as the 'forgotten county'. City folks always seem to hurry through it on the main roads, with the beckoning attractions of Devon and Cornwall more prominent in their minds. In literary terms, Dorset found a certain amount of fame in the late 19th century, thanks to the inspired novels of Thomas Hardy, who used the country charm of Dorset to form a framework for several of his works. The fictional town of Casterbridge had been based on Dorchester, the county town, and the lives and trials of country folk had found their way into *Tess of the D'Urbervilles*. The vales and rolling green scenery was a prime example of what the British Tourist Association liked to put on posters and promote around the world, tempting foreign visitors to come to Britain for their holidays.

Stuart drove the car up to a major viewpoint and beauty spot, named Hardy's Monument, where Horace was waiting for them.

Bonnie was first out of the car and went off to relieve herself. Horace greeted everyone, and went on to tell Hector that, contrary to what he had assumed, the Hardy to which the monument referred was not Thomas Hardy, but Vice-Admiral Hardy, who had supported Nelson at the Battle of Trafalgar, earning himself a place in history as being the subject of Nelson's alleged dying quote, "Kiss me, Hardy."

They walked around the base of the tower – a folly, built and paid for by local people in tribute to Vice-Admiral Hardy – and then took in the view across the sea, looking at the shingle bank that stretched along the shoreline from Portland in the distance.

"This was a major smugglers' landing zone during the 18th and 19th centuries," Horace explained. "Boats laden with French brandy would be rowed ashore in the middle of the night, and the local smugglers would be able to tell exactly where they were merely by scooping up a handful of shingle from the shore. You see, from all the way down there in Portland, along the coast here, the size of the pebbles goes from large to small, so, wherever you land, you can gauge the location by the size of the pebbles. It's the result of thousands of years of tidal erosion, and it's the longest shingle bank in the world."

Barbara unpacked flasks of tea and coffee, the sandwiches and some cold cooked chicken, which everyone feasted on.

It was while Horace was gnawing away at a chicken leg that a thought struck him. "Have you had a closer look at your tea caddy, Hector?" Licking his fingers, Hector had to admit that he had not.

"Well, I'd suggest you do. I found a hidden compartment – empty, of course – but, who knows? You should check it out. Thomas could have put anything in there."

Hector laughed, and agreed that his brother was capable of such a trick. He and Stuart promised Horace they would make a point of taking a good look at the caddy when they got home. The idea of a hidden compartment hadn't crossed either's mind, but the possibility was there.

"People back then loved hiding precious things for their loved ones to seek out," Stuart said as they waved goodbye to Horace, who drove away down the hill, tooting his car horn as he went. "Maybe he's got a point. It's the kind of thing Dad would have done."

They drove through the stunning countryside during the afternoon, and, despite the winter's breath over the landscape, it looked cosy and snug. Thatched stone cottages looked warm and inviting, and, as the car drove along the ridge of a valley, wisps of smoke curled their way lazily from squat chimneys up into the sky.

The daylight was fading as they got home, and both Hector and Stuart admitted, with a thank you to Barbara, that it had indeed been a good idea for a day out. Even Bonnie felt revitalised, and bobbed along contentedly at Stuart's heels.

Barbara fixed three whiskies, and together they all sat around the dining-room table looking at the tea caddy.

Stuart picked it up, turning it around in his hands, studying each side and the base for a clue.

Barbara held it in one hand, gauging the weight as if the caddy were a bag of sugar. She then gave it a good shake, which revealed nothing, much to her frustration.

Hector left the table for a brief while, returning with the thin papers that Horace had given him. "Let's see if the maker wrote anything down, or if Lord whoever specified anything out of the ordinary."

Apart from the snuffling sounds coming from under the table, where Bonnie had set up camp, all three remained silent while Hector read the faded commission from His Lordship, and the bill sent with the completed caddy from Henry Weald & Son, written in the precise and sloping style of the time.

"Well?" said Barbara, as she put out a cigarette and promptly lit up another one. "Is there something? Could Tommy have hidden a surprise for us to find?"

Hector raised his eyebrows, thinking with an expression of 'Hmmm, let's see, shall we?' before he removed the lid and pulled out the pewter centrepiece, which would have held loose tea. The inside of the caddy was bland compared to the workmanship done on the outside. It was only on close scrutiny that Hector discovered a dovetail corner at the bottom of the caddy was made of a lighter shade of wood. He took a pen from the table, and, using the nib, pushed tightly into the corner of the base, carefully making sure it was only the lighter wood he was putting any pressure on. The caddy at this point gave up, and, at last, half of the base slid across to reveal a hidden space under the false base.

Hector gasped, Barbara twitched, and Stuart shuffled his feet. Before anyone could say anything, Hector emptied the caddy out on to the tablecloth. At least a dozen perfectly cut diamonds spilled across the table, settling around the bottom of a ketchup bottle.

Nobody moved for what seemed like a long time, though in truth it was only a minute at most. Finally, Barbara looked from the gems to the caddy, to Stuart and to Hector, saying nothing more than, "Well, I'll be . . . " before sitting back in the chair, and gulping back the whisky left in her tumbler.

Stuart paused for a moment, and, sitting down, folded his arms and asked, "So, then, Mr Hector Barnes, gem dealer from Singapore, what can you tell us about these little darlings?"

Hector gathered the stones into the centre of the table with a cupped hand, and, picking each one up, held them between his thumb and forefinger. "The cut is exquisite – that's one thing for certain – and each stone is perfection. There are no small ones. They're all made to the same size, but, more importantly, let me show you something." Laying four diamonds on the table side by side carefully, he drew Barbara and Stuart's attention to the colour of each stone. "Not all diamonds are clear or white. Due to the carbon effects when the diamond is created by nature, you get a tint of colour in some diamonds. There are pink ones, like the one used in the movie *The Pink Panther*. However, you also get blue, green, and turquoise diamonds – these four for example." Pointing with a shaking finger, Hector drew Stuart towards the stones. "Look – a white one, a blue, then a green and finally pink. Every one is perfect in clarity. That's just four of them; the others are equally marvellous."

Barbara leaned over the table. "You make them sound like snooker balls – blue, green, pink. Does the colour make them less valuable than the clear ones?"

Hector sighed, taking a handkerchief out of his pocket and wiping his hands and brow. "No, Barbara, if anything it increases the value

– especially the blue and green ones. They are particularly rare. At a rough and conservative estimate, you are looking at nearly a million pounds worth of diamonds."

This time, it was for more than a minute that everyone sat speechless around the table looking at the sparkling gems in front of them, hearing Hector's voice in their heads saying the words 'million pounds' over and over.

Eventually, Barbara got to her feet with the words, "Well, this won't get the sprouts boiled, will it?" She went off to the kitchen, leaving Stuart studying a blue diamond, and playing with it in his hand.

"I have to wonder, and ask," Hector said carefully, "where would Thomas have got these from? Do you have any ideas?"

Stuart thought for a moment, his brow furrowed. "He did know a couple of antique dealers from Holland at one point, but that was years ago. He went over for a few fairs and sales, but came back with nothing in particular. I remember him saying what pointless trips they had been, and that when it came to quality antiques this country was the dog's doodahs. You get the picture? He never mentioned anything about these, but perhaps, giving him the benefit of any doubt, he bought them one at a time over a long period, and kept them hidden safe for the future assurance of comfortable living."

Hector poured another drink. "Well, he'd have had to sell some pretty expensive antiques to afford these gems. As to what we are going to do with them, well, we will have to give that some serious thought. It's not exactly as if you could go into the jeweller's shop on the high street and scatter these in front of him with the words, 'Make me an offer,' is it?"

Stuart agreed, as Barbara returned and began laying the table for the evening meal.

"Move them, please," she said impatiently. "I don't want them lying all over the place, they make me feel nervous. We can't keep them under this roof for very long either. Any ideas?"

Steak and kidney pie with Brussels sprouts and potatoes boiled to death was consumed amidst an air of brain cells working overtime. In three days' time they would all be on their way to Singapore, so something had to develop before then.

Hector finished his meal, and, after closing up the false base of the caddy, replaced the pewter centrepiece and lid, and put the caddy back in his room. The diamonds, they all agreed, could rest for the time being in the plastic pineapple on top of the bar in the corner of the Elvis lounge.

Hector had a knock on his bedroom door early the next morning, and

66

Stuart entered, followed by Bonnie, who hopped onto his bed and curled up in what she had found to be a warm spot next to his thigh. Stuart perched on the end of the bed and smiled confidently.

Hector rubbed his eyes, yawned, and propped himself up on his elbow. "So? Why the smile? Have you discovered a solution?"

Stuart sniffed, crossed his legs and looked intently at Hector. "Listen, Mum is very uncomfortable with these in the house. To be frank, we need the money, and, lovely as they are, looking at beautiful diamonds won't redecorate the Bide-a-Wee, or buy me a car. So, we should sell them, which leads me to think that the best place for that would be through your company in Singapore. We can take them with us, sell them, and transfer the money from Singapore back to Mum's bank account here."

Hector smiled back at Stuart. "You haven't had much sleep thinking that little lot out, have you? It's an admirable plan, except for one thing. You can't just walk into Singapore, through Changi Airport customs, with a pocketful of a million pounds worth of diamonds. You realise, of course, that there are limitations on imports there. We could courier them there. I know someone in London who could take care of that, but, even then, it'll draw attention where we don't want it. We're going to have to smuggle them in somehow – no shingle pebbles to help us either!"

They laughed, and returned to thinking about how it could be done.

Barbara listened intently to their plan, and spent an hour or so taking up the hem on a skirt she'd bought in a jumble sale at the local church hall. She was no five-star seamstress, but doing an activity such as this gave her the clear head she needed to think things through. So biting off the thread at the end of the task, she folded the skirt, flipped the lid of her needlework basket, and announced, "I've got it!" to the surprised faces who had been sat pensively in front of the television watching a quiz show, where contestants competed for a top prize of a million pounds.

It was all a bit surreal, watching these nervous people from Middle England answer questions for all that money, when next to them was probably the most expensive plastic pineapple ice bucket ever known.

"Now then," Barbara said, whilst she was unwrapping a bar of chocolate on the sofa, "I think Tinkie should come to Singapore too. That being the case, we'll need to take a frock or two, the wig, and some of that drag jewellery you've got in the vanity case, Stuart."

"Why?" asked Stuart. "I'm not planning on doing any shows there."

Barbara worked a chunk of chocolate around her mouth, and, pushing it into her cheek, carried on: "I know that, and Hector knows that, but they won't, will they? Who made your last sequined special, Stuart?"

He thought for a moment, and said, "It was Candy O'Keefe. Lovely old queen, retired from the drag circuit, but runs a fab costume repair and dressmaking business from his home in Brighton. Mum, I know where you're going on this one, and I'm with you all the way." Hector looked confused, so Stuart elaborated. "I'll give Candy a bell, tell her we're going down for a bit of frock repair work and to spruce up a neckline. After the job's done, and the diamonds are sewn onto the neckline of a sparkling sequined frock, pop it into a suit carrier, and off we go to Singers. The gems won't look out of place on a drag frock, and if anyone asks, they're all fake, just like everything else on the dress. Thanks to the sparklers everywhere else, they'll fit right in. Nobody would think that a drag queen's costume is made with REAL gems! After all, everything else is zirconia or paste, and just looks snazzy. It's all in the illusion, which is, in fact, part of the drag thing anyway, wouldn't you agree, Hector?"

Hector pursed his lips, nibbled his bottom lip for a few seconds, and concurred. "I like it. It will work, especially as the stones are all different colours. You're right about the illusion. Mixed with all the other stuff, they'll look tacky."

Raising an eyebrow, Stuart asked, "Are you saying Tinkie is tacky?"

"Only in a theatrical, gold-plated way. Just how a drag queen ought to be, isn't it? You haven't exposed me to that world for nothing!"

Hector and Barbara laughed heartily, and Stuart conceded the fact. He went to the hallway and phoned Candy O'Keefe to let him know they would be on his doorstep the next morning.

The following morning, it was Hector who came through the front door just after nine, Bonnie in tow, and with a broad smile on his face.

"What have you been up to?" asked Barbara as she helped a fried egg out of the pan and onto a slice of toast.

"I've hired a car. It makes sense really. We can use it to go to Brighton to see Candy wotsit, and then from there we can all go up to Heathrow for the flight home, and drop off the car at the airport. The young lady at Avis was most helpful."

"Excellent plan, love," smiled Barbara as she teased some egg onto a fork. "I was thinking it would be a lot of lost time and hassle to go everywhere by train. Besides, you can't rely on the timetable for the changeover at Southampton. As for using the car to go up to the airport, a brilliant idea, Stuart will be pleased." She then concentrated on spreading the oozing egg yolk over the toast, and enjoying her breakfast.

They drove along the coast to Brighton, and arrived outside a terraced house near the seafront just before eleven. Stuart pulled a suit carrier out of the car boot, and, together with Barbara and Hector, they stood on the front step and rang the doorbell, which chimed the chorus of 'Edelweiss' from *The Sound of Music.*

The door opened, and there stood Candy O'Keefe. He was a short man, aged somewhere in his mid- to late seventies, with heavy eyelids, hardly any eyebrows at all, and just a few wisps of thin hair all teased with lots of hairspray to give a candyfloss look. The blue rinse didn't help, but it obviously made Candy feel better about his appearance, and nobody was about to criticise his style since stories of his razor-sharp tongue from years on the cabaret circuit were legion. He had retired only about five or six years ago, and, since then, made a small living from the repair and exaggeration of some already extravagant drag artistes' costumes.

They all sat in his lounge, while he served coffee in a Royal Albert coffee service, and sliced up a sponge cake, made the second he had come off the phone from Stuart the night before.

"It's so nice to see you, dear," he said as he stirred his coffee. "You're looking so well, and it's lovely to meet you at last, Barbara. This must be a bit different from the Far East for you, Hector, but I hope you're having a good time. More cake?"

Hector took a slice, mindful of the good intention and wonderful manners being exuded. Life in Candy's home seemed to be almost a step into the past. The decor was not overly fluffy, which had surprised him. Apart from the over-tanned Spanish flamenco-dancer doll on the mantelpiece, flourishing in her traditional costume, everything was rather nice and stylish.

Stuart unzipped the suit carrier, and showed Candy what he wanted done. "Can you put these sparklers around the neckline on this frock, dear. I think it'll add that little something extra to the tired old thing."

Handing over a paper bag with the gems in it, they all held their breath while Candy looked at the neckline of the frock. He took out a stone from the bag, holding it next to the material. "Yes, I reckon it can be done, and will certainly help the frock, but I can't say it'll help the act!"

They laughed nervously.

"When do you need this done by? I've got to glue clasps onto these before I can sew them around the neck."

Stuart tried to appear as blasé as he could, but had to impress the urgency on Candy that it was a job of high importance. "I've got a job to do tomorrow night in London, so I'll need it finished by lunchtime, or mid-afternoon at the latest. I'll pick it up from you, and go directly up to London and wear it for the show."

Candy placed his cup and saucer on the coffee table almost without a sound, and looked at Stuart. "You do see I'm no chicken, dear, don't you, as much as I would wish to be. I don't have the stamina or speed to do a job that fast. Also – and you know this of old, Stuart – I take time to do a job properly. It can't possibly be done."

Hector leaned forward and said quietly, "We'll pay you two hundred pounds cash."

Candy swallowed hard. "Three o'clock okay?"

They left Candy selecting a tape of *Oklahoma* to sing along to while he worked.

After a short lunch break of fish and chips on the pier, they drove back to Boscombe, and began packing for the trip to Singapore.

Hector took a taxi back to Bob and Vicky, where he had to retrieve his suitcase and other clothes, which had been stored in the cupboard under the stairs.

Bob was, as Hector had expected, discreet. The same could not be said of Vicky, who had more questions than a Gestapo officer at an interrogation with the clock ticking.

Keeping the taxi waiting outside ensured Hector of a reasonably quick getaway, but not before he had pressed Bob for the promise of a trip to Singapore, where he would relish the opportunity to pay back their help and generosity at what had been such a difficult time.

Bob shrugged his shoulders. "But that's what friends do for each other, isn't it? We go way back, so just accept the fact that all I wanted was to make things easy and straightforward for you. As for coming to Singapore, I'd love to, but it's getting her to sit still on a jumbo for twelve hours that's the problem. She's petrified of getting a DVT on a two-hour flight to Spain." Walking out to the taxi, he hugged Hector and then smiled. "Bugger it! We'll come. I'll just tell her it's all sorted, and we'll come out there in a few months' time."

Hector got in the taxi and, closing the door, said, "That would be fantastic. I mean it, Bob. Please come; it'll do you good, and Vicky can do tours and sightseeing to her heart's content. We'll talk on the phone nearer the time."

That settled, the taxi drove away, and Hector kicked himself for not asking Bob to bring Bernie too when they came to Singapore – if they came. You never knew with some folks – good intentions and all that – but out of sight, out of mind was a bad habit for such good friends as they were to harbour. He hoped they would make it some day.

Back at the Bide-a-Wee, both Barbara and Stuart were in a frenzy of folding clothes, stuffing socks and underwear inside shoes, and delving into the back of the airing cupboard to retrieve the coolest and lightest of nightwear. Hector had understated the Singapore climate and humidity by telling them it would be hot and steamy. This seemed to draw the right reaction, for they were packing anything lightweight, and even found a small fan to take.

"It's amazing some of the rubbish she keeps," said Stuart, "but this time I have to admit she's come up trumps. A week in Malta, nearly ten years ago, and now the present comes into its own." With a twist of his wrist, he unfurled the fan depicting a print of Valletta harbour and began fanning himself furiously.

Hector smiled. "We do have air conditioning there you know, and they also sell fans. What's happening to Bonnie while you're away?"

Barbara pushed past them on the landing with a pile of towels in her grip. "She's going to the vicar and his wife. I spoke to them at the church-hall jumble sale, and they said they'd love to have her to stay for a couple of weeks. She knows them too, so there's no danger of the local press being full of stories about clergy being savaged by a half-crazed pug. The reverend will pick her up in the morning, and then we can drive to Brighton, collect the dress, and go on up to Heathrow. What time's the plane?"

Hector checked the tickets, and confirmed that it was a ten o'clock take-off, so they would need to check in by eight at the latest.

Barbara decided that the vicar and his wife would be the best bet, since not only would they take good care of Bonnie, but would also keep an eye on the Bide-a-Wee. After all, in this day and age if you couldn't trust the Church, who could you trust?

The day of departure dawned with a thick blanket of fog covering the town. In the distance you could even hear the faint wail of a foghorn out at sea. They all ate a full breakfast, using up nearly everything in the fridge. A box of dog food and biscuits was ready, along with a favourite toy or two, and Bonnie was sat on her chair in the Elvis lounge expecting something nasty to happen at any moment.

The doorbell rang, and a very well wrapped-up vicar presented himself for the collection of one small dog and a set of house keys. Bonnie had to be coaxed off her throne, and eventually set off with the vicar, both of them disappearing quickly into the foggy street.

"We should set off as soon as possible," said Hector, concerned about the time. "It'll take longer to get clear of this fog and along to Candy's. Are you both ready? Passports? Luggage?"

Stuart came downstairs with his lilac vanity case. "What about plane tickets? Where do we get them?"

"Don't panic," Hector explained calmly. "My assistant in Singapore has organised for us to collect them from the desk at Heathrow."

Barbara stood in the hall, buttoned up her coat, tied a headscarf under her chin and, with her little finger, traced around the edge of her mouth, tidying lipstick smudges. "Right then, are we off?" she said to both men, whom she addressed in the mirror.

As if by command, they packed the car and set off slowly, with Stuart cursing the weather conditions as they went.

They stopped on the way to Brighton for a short break.

"Coffee, cigarettes, and a quick pee is all I'm asking for," pleaded Stuart.

Pulling into a service station, they sat on plastic moulded chairs and drank their coffee, watching families squabbling by the hot trays, where people were being grossly overcharged for the poor excuse of food that was on offer.

Arriving at Candy's, after they had left the fog behind just past Portsmouth, Stuart checked the dress, counted the gems to himself around the neck of the costume and zipped up the suit carrier, which signalled to Hector that all was as it should be.

"It's a wonderful job, as always, my darling. Thanks ever so. They'll love it tonight."

Hector handed over an envelope with the cash inside it, and Candy counted it.

"Not to appear rude, love, but business is business. I've always counted my wages, so you'll not change me now. Where are you performing tonight that needed such a rush job anyway?"

Stuart fumbled for words briefly, before launching into a long monologue about the forces needing a new sweetheart, and tonight Tinkie would be entertaining the troops near the Palace, and he'd been pre-warned to expect their commander-in-chief to show up for the show.

"Not HMQ, surely?" wheezed Candy, clutching his hand to his chest in a dramatic fashion as befitted a retired drag queen.

"My lips are sealed," smiled Stuart sweetly. "Nevertheless, I'm in no doubt that the frock will be appreciated."

As they pulled away in the car, Hector asked, "Why did you bring the Queen into it?"

Stuart beamed back at him. "If one mentions HMQ in regard to performances, and the forces to boot, you're pretty much guaranteed a modicum of confidentiality, at least from Candy. The Official Secrets Act, the threat of a dawn raid, or even a Royal rebuff is enough to keep her lips buttoned."

Barbara passed round some buttered buns. "Made at home, not

bought at that awful place where we had coffee, so don't worry – they're rather nice."

Presently, they arrived at Heathrow, dropped off the hire car, and caught a shuttle bus to the terminal, where they collected their tickets and went to the check-in counter.

"Are those flowers real?" Barbara asked, nodding in the direction of the top of the counter.

"They are, indeed," replied Hector. "I didn't mention it earlier, but, now that we're all here, you may as well know that I always travel in business class or first, but never economy. Not on long-haul flights – the extra space and comfort are so vital for such a long trip. Besides, the trimmings are always quite good."

"Quite good?" squawked Stuart. "My suitcase has just been given a priority tag. It's never had a priority anything before. Neither, for the record, have Mum or I. This is going to be lovely, I just know it."

With that, and boarding passes collected, they went through the fast-track security check, and aimed for the executive lounge for drinks before boarding.

Stuart had held onto the suit carrier, telling the check-in agent he was a drag queen, and that the precious frock would not be leaving his side. The lady from Singapore Airlines had courteously and professionally handled the situation, assuring Stuart that there would be no problem. The suit carrier could be stowed in a wardrobe on board the aircraft, and she even handed him a Raffles class tag to place over the hanger.

The service was impeccable, and, in the lounge, with a relaxed atmosphere and a selection of canapés to choose from, Barbara finally let her shoulders down, removed her headscarf and, looking at Hector, said, "This really is a big treat for us. You're spoiling us already, and we haven't even left London yet. You certainly know what appeals to Stuart. You've come a long way since first meeting us, don't you think?"

Hector popped a cracker and some cheese into his mouth, nodding in agreement. "I don't think I would ever have got my head around all this had it not been for your guidance and Stuart's persistence showing me that the life you've got is a good one. But let's not kid each other – when we complete things in Singapore, life will be as Thomas always planned for you: more comfortable, and with the chance to enjoy each day without having to hope for guests to cross your doorstep in order for you to make a living. As for Stuart's lifestyle and line of work, yes, I admit I had very serious misgivings in the beginning. Don't hold that against me. I was – still am – a stickler for tradition. However, I will freely declare to you now that having watched and listened, not only to Stuart but also to the people around him, I am proud of him. It's not as easy as people think to do the work that he does. Usually the venues and changing areas he uses are not exactly to his desire, yet he still gets on with it. That is what reminds me of myself at his age, and where we connect. Besides which, he's got a taste for the expensive things in life, just like his uncle."

"You're right there," smiled Barbara. "It's what Tommy always said about him: he's got champagne taste and beer money."

Stuart returned to the comfortable lounge chairs and sofa with a plate piled high with a selection of nearly every canapé that had been on offer. Champagne fizzed in a flute glass, and, for the first time in a very long time indeed, Stuart felt that he had found his niche. This was where he belonged.

The lounge hostess made an announcement that the flight was ready for boarding, so, with Hector leading the way, they boarded the aircraft and were guided to their seats by the world-renowned crew that were the signature of the airline's enviable reputation.

The flight attendant assured Stuart that the suit carrier would be well cared for, but he followed her to the wardrobe anyway. Only after she had showed him where the frock had been put, and invited him to check it whenever he wished during the flight, did he calm down and enjoy the space and comfort that the business-class seat afforded him.

The aircraft roared down the runway, heaving itself into the sky, and banked over Windsor, turning north-east towards the coast, and climbed through the thick winter clouds.

Picking out the twinkling lights below, Hector took a moment to quietly bid farewell to Thomas. He got out a book he had bought at Heathrow to read on the flight.

Barbara chose a couple of magazines that the crew offered, and began chatting to the businessman next to her, who, to her immediate and loud delight, was an Australian. He was young too, which made her want to mother him, but she managed to hold back her maternal feelings, which was a huge relief to him also.

After dinner had been served, and he had watched a movie on his personal screen, Stuart leaned across the aisle and asked Hector, "Are we there yet?" To which he was told to watch another three or four movies, and by then they would nearly be there.

The crew circulated with a selection of liqueurs and brandy, so Stuart chose a fine cognac, made friends with several glasses, and went to sleep for a few hours, helped by the marshmallow comfort of his seat.

Waking up for more food, all three of them chatted about how Bonnie would be settling in, and if she had made the vicar's wife swear like a sailor yet.

After the long journey, the plane descended over the city. Eventually it banked over the harbour, showing Barbara a view of all the boats and oil tankers that were anchored for the night.

The jumbo kissed the ground, and, slowing down, pulled off the runway, gracefully making its way to the terminal.

"That was such a lovely trip, I don't want to get off," said Barbara, "but since there's so much waiting here for me, I'd better."

The Australian smiled. "You could always come on to Sydney with me."

Barbara giggled girlishly, and caught a glance from Stuart that told her all she needed to know.

The flight attendant brought the suit carrier to Stuart, and thanked him for flying with Singapore Airlines as he stepped off the aircraft. This was a nice change from the charter flights to Spain, which he had been used to up until now.

"I'm not a snob," he said to Hector as they walked up the air bridge, "I simply appreciate the finer things in life."

"I couldn't have put it better myself," Hector acknowledged, and steering Barbara between them, who was saying that despite the foot rest, she wished she had worn some more comfy shoes because her ankles had swollen a bit, they made their way to the baggage reclaim area. They loaded up two trolleys with their cases, and spread the suit carrier on top, before heading towards the customs channel.

The customs official's gaze was drawn to the lilac vanity case swinging from Stuart's arm. Men didn't travel with such items, so this deserved a few questions.

"Welcome to Singapore. Would you come over here for a moment please," he instructed. Guiding a trolley, he pulled it to one side of the stream of passengers who were all meandering through the channel as though they were tainted with the same streak of guilt. "What is the purpose of your visit to Singapore?" the official asked, eying all three of the passengers in front of him – a mature, distinguished gentleman, resident in Singapore: a middle-aged lady, not used to wearing her best clothes, and with shoes that were too tight; and a young, rather effeminate man, who was watching him almost as much as he was them.

"I live here," answered Hector, "and this is my sister-in-law and nephew, both of who are here for the first of what I hope will be many visits."

The official nodded. "Can I see inside the small case, please?" and he pointed to the vanity case, which Stuart merrily passed to him.

"Help yourself, but I don't think anything will suit you!" he laughed, and regretted it almost instantly.

The official didn't smile, let alone laugh. He opened the case, which revealed a collection of Stuart's drag jewellery. "Is this real?" he asked, his face growing more quizzical.

"Good Lord, no!" gasped Stuart. "I'm a female impersonator cabaret artiste. That's just my costume jewellery, my wig and shoes are in the suitcase and my frock's on top in the carrier. I'm here for a performance."

The official nodded again, and asked, "Do you hold a permit to work in Singapore?"

Stuart opened his mouth, but nothing came out. Hector coughed, and said discreetly to the official, "It's a private function to be held at my home – a birthday party – and my nephew will be performing to an invited audience. No fee – family affair – you know the kind of thing."

The official sighed. He didn't know the kind of thing, nor wanted to, but if it was within the privacy of this man's home, he wasn't going to hold things up. The lady had gone pale – probably the long flight – so closing their passports, and taking his hand off the suit carrier, he finished with, "Okay, enjoy Singapore, and the party. Thank you. You may proceed."

They wheeled the trolleys through the sliding doors to where Alex was stood waiting for them. Trying their hardest not to walk faster than what would appear normal, they went outside to where the car was waiting.

Alex loaded up the car with the luggage, and, after Hector had made the introductions, assisted Barbara into the car. Alex offered to take the suit carrier from Stuart, who, on a cue from Hector, let it go in the boot with the cases.

With the air con on full blast, Alex drove them to Hector's home, a penthouse apartment with views across the Singapore river, where, for the first time in several hours, they all heaved a huge sigh and fell onto a lounge sofa laughing together with the sheer relief of having arrived safely.

"If only Candy could see us now!" squealed Stuart, and they all toasted him with some chilled champagne that Jean had left for them in the bar fridge.

Although it was late evening, the temperature and humidity were still both high. As they all stood on Hector's balcony, which ran in an L shape around the penthouse, finishing the champagne and looking at the view of the city, Hector enlightened Barbara and Stuart on the city laid out and twinkling before them.

"I'll get Jean, my assistant, to advise you on some city sightseeing tours. We can all go across to Sentosa on the cable car for a day. There's a nice beach there. Also, we have to have tiffin at the Raffles Hotel one afternoon. It's one of the nicest and most traditional things one can do when in Singapore. Does all that appeal to you two?"

Barbara swallowed the last of her champagne, puffed her cheeks out and dabbed her brow with a small handkerchief. "Yes, it all sounds marvellous. The only thing that concerns me is the humidity. It's quite draining, and it will take me a while to get used to. Even though Spain and Malta were warm when we went, they were nothing like this heat."

Stuart nodded in agreement, adding, "I'm sure we'll adjust in a day or two. Anyway, what's tiffin? and when do we do something about those diamonds on the frock?"

Hector sat in one of his high-backed wicker chairs, and, brushing some imaginary dust off his knee, thought for a few moments. "Well, tiffin is another word for afternoon tea. The Raffles Hotel is the premier hotel here, and has followed the high colonial standards for years now. Tiffin is sheer decadence. I know you'll enjoy it. We must call and book a table, as it gets very busy with tourists on short visit time frames. Luckily, I know the concierge at the hotel, so I've no doubt he'll be able to make a reservation for us. As for the diamonds, I'll talk it over with Jean at the office. Having got them here, the next thing is to drum up some interest from potential buyers. It's going to have to be a bit on the hush-hush – after all, their source is somewhat original, wouldn't you say?" He smiled, inviting Stuart to sit down.

Barbara had by now stretched herself out on a chaise longue, which was strategically placed under a whirling ceiling fan. "I don't see what's so cloak-and-dagger about it – after all, they were an inheritance, so that's legal and above board, isn't it?" she said, as, with a bit of effort, she kicked her shoes off and twiddled her toes.

"It's not that aspect of the situation that perplexes me," Hector mused. "It's just that now they're here – and we really ought to have declared them, owing to their value – we have to choose our buyer carefully."

"I guess in some circles they'd be what's known as 'hot ice', wouldn't they?" laughed Stuart. Yawning, and stretching his arms before folding his hands behind his head, he let out a deep and contented sigh. "Oh, but it's lovely to be somewhere so exotic, and I've no doubts that Uncle Hector here will know a few shady folks who would be only too pleased to part with a couple of million for such stunning gems."

Hector merely smiled back. He got up to take his suitcase to his room, where he started unpacking. He showed his guests to their rooms, and after a group hug, which to their surprise, they all admitted had been quite nice, they went to sleep.

Chapter Five

Asian Encounter

Jean stood on the platform of the metro station. Despite it being still early morning, the start of the commuter rush to work was evident, and there was hardly any room in which to open a newspaper, which annoyed her. She had enjoyed the luxury of having Alex and the car ferry her around town while Hector had been away, but, of course, like all good things, it had come to an end with the boss's return home. So now she would have to get used to travelling around the city just like everyone else did. The journey was short, but just long enough for her to do the crossword in the morning paper.

She stopped briefly to pick up a croissant and espresso from one of the European chains of cafés in the vast expanse of a shopping mall. She then made her way to the Oriental Gem Emporium, where she greeted the security officer sweetly but briskly, before making her roost for the day at her desk outside Hector's office.

An hour later, with the mail sorted and added to a file for Hector to peruse when he arrived, she was just powdering her nose and chin when the lift door pinged. Out walked Hector, followed by a small woman oozing with British regional character, and a willowy young man, who flounced past her as if he owned the place. She didn't know who to be most surprised at, but, waiting only a few seconds for Hector to be seated at his desk, she picked up the post file and went into the office, pushing her small butterfly-shaped hairgrip firmly into place.

"So, how was the rest of your trip? I'm so sorry about Thomas – it must have been a terrible shock." Turning to Barbara and Stuart, she announced, "Good morning. I'm Jean, Mr Barnes's assistant. Welcome to Singapore. How long will you be staying?"

Barbara sniffed and looked at the various works of art that adorned the office walls. Stuart stood and, extending a hand, said, "We're not sure how long – probably a couple of weeks. I'm Stuart, by the way, Hector's nephew and Thomas's son. This is my mother, Barbara. Say hello, Mother."

Barbara looked up at Jean and, almost in a whisper, said, "Hello. Pleased to meet you."

She couldn't work out in her mind why she felt so insignificant when faced with the imposing figure of Jean. As it was, whilst it appeared to her that Stuart certainly had no qualms and was being the essence of introductory niceness here in Hector's office, Barbara simply felt uncomfortable and, more to the point, inferior. This was an emotion that didn't sit easily with her. She fumbled around in her handbag and produced a packet of duty-free cigarettes. Looking up, she realised everyone had stopped talking and was looking at her.

"The whole complex is a non-smoking area," remarked Jean.

Hector got up from his leather desk chair, moved round to the front of the large desk, perched on the corner and folded his hands on his knee. "One thing you will notice very quickly here in Singapore, is that there are certain laws which may seem out of place elsewhere in the world, but, with the growing mood sweeping across continents, you will understand that it's actually a sign of the times. Singapore simply set its own standard a few years ago: no smoking in public places, offices or restaurants. If you happen to have a smoke in the street and stub out your butt on the pavement or kerbside, it's more than likely that a citizen will approach you and tell you off, pointing at the offending cigarette butt and telling you to pick it up. They don't go a whole lot on litter either. Whilst I'm on the subject, chewing gum is also illegal here. It seems that someone stuck a piece of gum on the doors of one of the metro trains, creating a problem that meant the doors would not close easily. There were delays on the train, which happened to be carrying a government minister to a meeting, for which he was late. So enraged was he, that he voiced his opinion in parliament, proposed a bill to ban chewing gum, and got it through."

Stuart was shocked, and said so. "So, then, no smokes, gum or litter? Sounds a bit of a police state to me."

Jean leaned against the desk. "Some see it that way, but on the whole it's a good place to live. The Singaporeans sell tee shirts and tourist goods which take the mickey out of all these laws. It's along the lines of 'Singapore's a fine place – a fine for this and a fine for that!' You'll see all that kind of thing on the tours."

Stuart handed her the leaflet. "I think we should do a tour to the Jurong Bird Park, Chinatown, and a half-day city tour."

Jean made notes. "Excellent choice! I always find that a city tour really helps one to get one's bearings in a new place, don't you, Barbara?"

Barbara nodded and managed a smile. When all was said and done, this woman was no different to her – just flesh and blood. So, deciding that this feeling of intimidation wasn't going to deter her one bit, Barbara stood up. "So, where exactly can I have a bloody fag, then?"

The following day, Stuart and Barbara were dropped off at the starting point for the city bus tour by Alex, and they joined a group of tourists for the tour. This gave Hector and Jean the first real opportunity to sit down together and have a morning's catch-up meeting.

The Italian jewellery designers were due into Changi in a couple of days. One of Hector's sales team had a breakfast meeting scheduled tomorrow with a wholesaler from Hong Kong, and Hector had been requested to join them.

"Finally," Jean added, with a light sigh of relief at having gone through the list she had compiled in Hector's absence, and taking a small sip of green tea, which they had both enjoyed throughout the meeting, "Lee Eng Tek wants to see you. He's coming from Manila on Thursday. He will be spending a few days here, and staying at the Raffles. He leaves Monday lunchtime for Jeddah. He won't say what he wishes to discuss, but sounded very insistent that he should see you."

Hector pondered for a few minutes, playing with one of those executive toys on his desk that Barbara had seen in a mail-order catalogue. "He may just be the person that I want to see, too. See if you can schedule a dinner meeting for Friday or Saturday. Book a table for six somewhere nice – somewhere different. I'll take Barbara and Stuart with me."

Jean's pen paused briefly.

"Don't worry," he said, noticing the break in her writing. "I want you to come too. When you hear what I'm going to propose, your input may be invaluable."

Jean's pen continued its trail. Shortly afterwards, Jean was winding the telephone cord around her fingers as she spoke with Mr Lee's secretary in Kuala Lumpur.

Although based there, it was well known that Lee Eng Tek spent most of his time travelling. Business on the trot was the favourite chosen method of his, and the chance to gain thousands of frequent flyer mileage points was always capitalised upon. Lee Eng Tek was a proud Malaysian, born of Chinese-rooted aristocracy. Though getting on in years, he had seen enough of life to be well prepared for whatever it threw at him. He had learnt a long time ago that to show mild indifference to what others would find shocking, distasteful or poor quality gave him an upper hand, for it meant that few ever really knew what affected him in any profound way. In business too this maxim had served him well. Westerners always said you could never tell what a Chinaman was really thinking. His face gave precious little away. So it had been, starting on a small scale selling Malaysian pewter, that he had gradually progressed over the years, amassing an empire along the way, with eyes and ears all across Asia, ready to tip him off at any moment when the chance of a good deal was up for grabs.

The only force to be met on such a scale was that of Hector Barnes. For someone of such pole-opposite origins, this man had developed a good oriental perspective on life, and, at several points over the years, he had managed to wield an upper hand in business against him. This, however, did not enrage Lee. It merely highlighted the fact that Hector was a competitor worthy of respect. Lee Eng Tek always made a point of speaking to him when in Singapore. By now they had a mutual respect and hidden fondness for each other. In recent times it had been to both their benefits for them to merge their sources on a couple of occasions, thereby getting a deal sorted and a decent profit to share. It was well known that if you needed to know something, or trace someone anywhere in the Far East, then it would be to Lee Eng Tek that you would turn. The one thing he had over Hector was a network of informers and spies that spread like a cobweb over the entire area, thus keeping Lee up to date with any new developments.

The fact that Hector had come back to Singapore with two people from England was a curiosity to him, so he made sure he was early to arrive at the Marina Mandarin Hotel's cocktail lounge, where it had been arranged that they would meet. As was always the case when meeting for business, he had Miss Lim with him.

Miss Lim was the Chinese equivalent of Jean. She was almost highbrow in an oriental fashion, discreet but meticulously attentive, and if crossed, deadly.

They sat in comfortable chairs, opposite a sofa and coffee table, sipping drinks and noting how much building work had taken place in the city since their last visit.

Hector and his party arrived punctually, thanks to Alex, met Lee and Miss Lim, and ordered cocktails as they reclined on the sofa. Lee permitted himself a small smile at these three sat on the sofa. It reminded him of the three monkeys: see all, hear all, and say nothing.

Stuart was completely agog, turning his head in all directions, taking in the surroundings of the impressive atrium lounge, and gazing out of the large window at Marina Bay, where tankers' lights twinkled back at him.

Hector introduced them to Lee as family, which Miss Lim quietly noted down, ready to add to the file on Hector, which took up so much space in her cabinet back in Kuala Lumpur.

Hector listened as Lee updated him on the various goings-on in Manila, not helped by the terrorist activity in the southern regions of the Philippines.

Barbara fished in her glass, chasing the cherry round and round until it got trapped between two ice cubes, and she teased it loose with a finger.

Jean watched in amazement, before turning to Miss Lim and enquiring after her health. She complimented Miss Lim on her bracelet, a thick band of pale, milky jade, which really wasn't to her own taste, but which she recognised to be valuable. She much preferred Mr Lee's vibrant green Burmese-jade cygnet ring. They had tried for a while now to get hold of some Burmese jade, as the emerald-green colour would have been perfectly suited to the order requested by the Italians. It had been passed back down the line that this type of jade was almost unobtainable due to the depleted stocks and source. Making eye contact with Hector, Jean drew his attention to the ring, and Hector gave a short nod as he popped a handful of nuts into his mouth.

Lee asked Barbara if they had visited Singapore before, drawing a nervous giggle and monosyllabic 'no' from her. He complimented Stuart on the sarong he was wearing.

"I saw the crew on the plane wearing them, and loved them. So, after our tour of the city this morning, I asked Hector's driver to take us somewhere I could buy some clothes, especially these things. Luckily they had almost the same batik print as the airline, so I was in heaven, wasn't I, Mother?"

Barbara grinned, inching to the edge of the sofa. "Oh yes! Stuart can make himself look great in almost anything. In fact, it makes a change to see him so nice in something other than sequins." She laughed heartily, and, passing a bowl to Jean, asked sweetly, "Nuts?"

Alex had brought the larger of Hector's cars out for the evening. This suited the group well for travelling together, but made the job of weaving through some of the more narrow streets a bit more difficult.

After cocktails, the group climbed into the car and, with Miss Lim nodding an acknowledgement to Alex, they set off for dinner.

Arriving in Little India, they got out of the car outside a restaurant entrance on Race Course Road.

"Ah, good selection, Jean," beamed Hector. "Barbara and Stuart should experience this, and I believe, Mr Lee, we conducted a bit of business over a meal here once before, did we not?"

"We did indeed, Mr Barnes," said Lee as he ushered the ladies in first, and upstairs to the dining area of the Banana Leaf Apollo – a famous restaurant that had been established for a long time and had earned itself a place on the 'off the trail' tourist trail.

Locals enjoyed it, and tourists loved the at-ease way of dining, and being presented with banana leaves instead of plates.

Stuart remarked, "How stunningly authentic this all is."

Looking at the menu, which spoke of many delights, but highlighted the well-known fish-head curry, Barbara opted for vegetarian curry, noting that, "I prefer to have food on the plate that doesn't look at me while I attempt to eat it."

This made everyone laugh, relaxed the atmosphere, and brought Hector and Lee round to the real reasons for their meeting.

"I hear you're going to Saudi Arabia on Monday," Hector said as he took a swig of his beer.

"That is correct," replied Lee, who was busy sucking on a fish head, making Barbara feel a bit sickly.

"Might I enquire as to the purpose of your trip? Are you buying or selling?" Hector was keen to establish this before continuing.

"You should know better than to ask that straight away. Why your haste? It's not usually your style." Lee wasn't going to lay down his cards that quickly – it spoiled the game and the chase.

"There's no haste," lied Hector, "merely the point that if you're selling, I may have something that will interest you – something so rare, in fact, that it is hardly ever advertised on the market. Were that to be the case, in fact, the supplier would be overwhelmed."

Lee's curiosity was now well and truly hooked. He had been in Manila trying to source a gift for a member of the Saudi royal family. There was to be a birthday celebration, hence his invitation to Jeddah. But, along with the invitation to the festivities came the request for a birthday gift to surpass all others – something spectacularly special and rare, as was the birthday girl herself, a beautiful desert princess. Lee reined in his thoughts, and began to calculate and concentrate. The client had said there was no ceiling in price, but it must be unique.

"Okay, then, Hector, tell me. What is it that's so rare and precious that has fallen into your hands? I can't imagine that it's legal, otherwise you wouldn't be sat here with me. But since I requested the meeting with your lovely Jean here, perhaps we can help each other."

Jean blushed and, excusing herself from the table, went to powder her nose with her trusty compact.

Wiping his hands on one of the hot towels provided for the table, Hector had to agree. "There's no doubt that we can help each other – of that I am certain. I have in my possession some diamonds – coloured diamonds."

This interested Lee. "How many exactly do you have?" he said, thinking that perhaps there would be three or four that could be used for earrings, or set in a ring.

"Approximately twenty of them, and all different colours too. I have verified them, and can tell you the asking price on behalf of my client is two million dollars."

Lee sipped on his iced tea, pausing only to give the impression that two million dollars would need some deep consideration, when in truth it didn't matter one bit.

Stuart and Barbara had by now realised that they were the client to whom Hector was referring, but, in keeping with his coolness, they focused on their kulfi. They ordered some watermelon juice, which, as they had both discovered since arriving, was very refreshing and tasted much better than the green tea which Hector still tried to tempt them with.

"Suppose that I am interested, and can raise the money. As I depart in two days' time, I need to see the stones, verify them for my own satisfaction, and have them packed ready to take with me to Jeddah." Lee looked deeply into Hector's face, reading his eyes, and recognised the same tiger instinct he had in himself.

Hector was calm in his response. "As for your own verification, I have no problems. In fact, when you see them you will notice that they are already packed, if that's the right word, for travelling. It may even suit you better than you realise. However, for myself, I need to ask for your help with some jade. You are the best person I know when it comes to getting good quality jade, but I need Burmese rather than Chinese. Can you help?"

Lee played with the ring on his finger. "I can help, of course. You know, I'm sure, how rare that particular strain of jade has become. But, I have my sources. When do you need it by?"

"Tuesday at the latest. I've got Italian designers coming in, and they want that vibrancy of green for their new line."

Miss Lim, who had quietly been scribbling away on a notepad, leaned over to Lee and whispered into his ear.

Jean returned to the table, and taking Hector's expression to mean that he was mid-negotiation, and seeing the amount of sweat pouring off Barbara and Stuart, realised it must be in regard to the diamonds that Hector had told her about at the end of their meeting when he had got back.

Simultaneously, both Jean and Miss Lim made notes as the two men spoke.

Barbara leaned over to Stuart and, masking her face with one of her small handkerchiefs, commented, "There's a lot of fannying going on. Are these two going to take for ever?"

"Dunno," he replied lazily. "Best let them get on with it, though – after all, it's for our future benefit."

What transpired from the meeting was an agreement that Lee Eng Tek would bring some jade to Hector's office on the Monday morning, and view the diamonds. If he was happy with them, he would take them with him to the airport, where he would take the one o'clock plane to Jeddah. Payment for the gems would be in cash, so Jean would arrange for an escort to go with her to the bank where she would deposit the money.

Hector had explained that in order to bring the diamonds into Singapore they had got them sewn around the neckline of a dress. Since it had worked to bring them in, there was no reason why it shouldn't work taking them out. Lee accepted this, thinking to himself that the Saudis may even like the idea of such precious gems adorning a dress that the princess could wear, and thereby impress all around her.

After dinner, having dropped Lee and Miss Lim back at the Raffles Hotel, Alex drove them home, before taking Jean home and then carrying on to meet friends for satay at a hawker's stall on Beach Road.

Sunday dawned steamily. Stuart lay on his bed, fanning himself with a cotton sheet, but taking little comfort, he got up and made a coffee. He went to sit on the balcony where he watched the city wake up. There was a scooter that buzzed by down below, with a couple clinging to each other, her hair flowing in the wind as he sped along with a picnic and other things on his mind. Across the road in a park, a group of elderly ladies were doing their morning t'ai chi exercises together. Two streets away, on the small balcony of an apartment block, he could see a young mother pegging laundry on to a washing line as she chatted to a giggling infant who was hiding between the clothes that were hung out to dry. It seemed that was the only time you could do this, as after a few hours the humidity would ensure that nothing hanging on a balcony would dry properly.

The sound of a toilet flushing announced that Hector was up, so Stuart boiled the kettle and made a cup of green tea.

They sat on the balcony doing the crossword in the *Straits Times* together, until about an hour later the morning calm was shattered by

85

Barbara having a good cough and making coffee for herself noisily in the kitchen.

"Right then," declared Hector. "How about a picnic on the beach today, folks? We'll take the cable car from Mount Faber across the harbour to Sentosa and find a nice spot on the beach."

Stuart smiled. "No Raffles there, then! That's all I hear – Raffles, Raffles, and more Raffles."

Hector realised, explaining, "Sir Stamford Raffles was the founder of Singapore in 1819 and from then he was instrumental in the setting up of Singapore as a major trading post. Consequently, you have many tributes to him today taking his name. The famous hotel, a large shopping mall, even the business class on Singapore Airlines is branded as Raffles class."

"Well, I'm glad we've cleared that up, then," Stuart said as he retreated to his room to shower and get ready for the excursion. "I thought all these people were obsessed with frothy clothes – you know, frills and all."

Barbara hacked up another cough. "That's ruffles, not Raffles!"

"It's the same thing," shrieked a voice from the shower room.

They took the cable car from the station on the summit of Mount Faber, Singapore's highest, or possibly only, peak.

Having sailed over the dockside, where a cruise liner was making ready for its departure, activating a lot of frantic movement along the dock, they arrived amid the lush vegetation of Sentosa Island. Traveller's palms fanned their leaves in welcome everywhere, and after Hector had hired bicycles, they cycled along the immaculately manicured pathways. They stopped at a relatively quiet stretch of beach, where they set up their picnic and sat in silence, eating the lunch that Barbara had prepared hastily before their departure that morning.

After sucking on a slice of fresh pineapple, and then picking strands of the fruit out of her teeth, Barbara pushed her sunglasses back up to the bridge of her nose and remarked, "My Tommy would have enjoyed this."

Stuart sighed and nodded in agreement. "He would indeed – even the theme park and flash hotel we saw when we got off the cable car. But this is lovely – a sandy beach, a picnic, and sunshine. It's a bit like Bournemouth on August Bank Holiday, really isn't it?"

Hector was looking down at the sand, which escaped and ran between his toes when he wiggled them. "It's such a shame he never came, but then, it begs the question that if he had come over at some point, would I have ever met you two? I suppose, in the end, it would have been inevitable that we would have been brought together. It just seems so sad that it's taken his death for us to meet up and get to know one another. I might as well say now that, despite a lifetime of having had fixed ideas about the way people should be in my eyes, you, Stuart, have opened my eyes in a big way. Even so, having come through those evenings beside you while you were working fairly unscathed, I realise that blood and family mean far more to me than I ever thought. So, all I guess I'm trying to say is that I'm glad Thomas brought us together, even though his method was rather unorthodox. Barbara, I would dearly like to see you relax a bit more at home when you go back. Maybe even sell the Bide-a-Wee and buy somewhere nice for you to live and for Bonnie to establish a new realm in. With the money from the diamonds, you should be able to manage that easily now."

Barbara, having finished her pineapple, was working busily with a wet wipe on her hands. Immediately afterwards, with the men watching in the curiously entranced way that men watch women attending to themselves, she proceeded to squirt a large dollop of suntan cream into the palm of her hand, and them spread it all over her legs, massaging the streaks of cream into skin, which, to be honest, was not used to tropical sunshine. As she rubbed away, she had a frown growing on her forehead.

"Penny for the thought?" enquired Hector.

"It will be okay tomorrow with Lee Eng Tek and the gems, won't it?" she asked.

Hector leaned over and rested on an elbow. "Of course it will. He's got his deadline to meet, and someone in Jeddah is waiting for a nice expensive birthday present. It was simply good timing on our part to have the goods that he had been scouring Asia for. He won't be inclined to hang around; he'll merely bring the money, take the dress, and go to the airport. When he does, Jean will go to the bank and deposit the money for you. She had the good sense to open an account for you, so you'll get cards and everything, which you can then use in England for – well, let's call them purchases. Does that relax you?"

Stuart got up and moved round to Barbara's side, putting his arm around her shoulders. "If he says it'll be fine, it will be. Now, give me a squirt of your cream and I'll do your shoulders."

Despite having reservations, for though she would never have admitted it Barbara didn't trust foreigners, she decided to let Hector handle the transaction, and therefore today would be a day of fun and relaxation. Settling on this thought, she lay back and picked up her copy of the latest Jilly Cooper novel, which she had started on the plane.

Stuart, already having come to the conclusion that Hector ought to be able to deal with the sale of a gem-encrusted frock without screwing it up, put on his Walkman, and lay back to crisp away in the sun, listening to *Erasure's Greatest Hits*.

Hector looked either side of him, and realised that for the moment, at least, there was nothing in common to be shared with these two. So, hauling himself to his feet, he went for a paddle along the lapping shoreline. A swim would have been nice, but, with an oil tanker moored offshore, it didn't exactly fill him with the urge to do so.

It was late afternoon when the three of them lazily got their things together, and cycled back to the hire point by the cable-car station, giggling most of the way. They took the cable car back to Mount Faber, where Alex met them and drove them home.

Dinner that evening was taken at Boat Quay. Sticks of chicken and beef sizzled away on the hawkers' stalls, and they feasted on satay, followed by what Hector assured them was a famous Singaporean speciality, namely chilli crab. This proved to be a roaring success, and they retired to bed that night relaxed, full and content.

The following morning dawned in the steamy and humid manner to which they had, by now, become accustomed. At least it had lived up to their expectations, for when reading about tropical places, even in what Stuart referred to as old books, like *Treasure Island*, the reader expects the location to be hot and sticky. Singapore fits this description on most days. They had breakfast together – one green tea and two coffees. Not a lot was spoken, but by now the three of them had grown comfortable enough in one another's company for them not to feel the need to say something to break a silence.

Hector mused on this, thinking that this was how it ought to feel.

Alex arrived promptly, as usual, and drove them to the Gem Emporium, where Jean greeted them. Taking a time check, she realised that she was going to enjoy this morning's activity, since it had a thrill attached to it which no other meeting until now had been able to match.

Miss Lim called to say that they were on their way, and to receive confirmation that the dress and jewels were ready.

Jean confirmed this, and mentioned that she trusted the finances had been arranged in order. Getting the all-clear on this front, she reported to Hector's office, in much the same way as the attending staff do to a general on a battlefield. Keeping an eye on the time, she powdered her face with the ever trusty compact, and set coffee and juices out on the conference table, just in case.

A call came through from the main gate to say that Lee and Miss Lim were just arriving in their car.

Jean calmly replaced the telephone, got up from her desk,

straightened her skirt, played with the cuffs on her shirt, and went into Hector's office with the air of a director backstage on first night. "They're here, so if you're all ready, then we're off." She just stopped short of clapping her hands and braying, 'Places, everyone, please,' but would have loved to have done so.

They were sat around a large conference table in the office when Jean ushered Lee Eng Tek and Miss Lim in, inviting them to take a seat at the table.

"Thank you for coming," said Hector. "I know you run to a tight schedule, no doubt thanks to the meticulous planning by Miss Lim here, but I am also aware that you have something we desire, as we in turn have something you need urgently."

With that, Stuart unzipped the suit carrier that lay on the table, and pulled out the sequined dress with the diamonds hanging from the neckline.

Lee Eng Tek leant forward, taking the dress from Stuart. He inspected the gems quietly, while everyone else sat in silence trying their hardest not to fidget. Some minutes later he motioned to Miss Lim, who produced an attaché case and placed it on the table. She flicked the locks and, turning the case towards Hector, displayed the neatly packed rows of bills.

"Two million, US. It's all there," Lee stated in a matter-of-fact manner. "Oh, and while I remember, in compliance with your other request, and as a gesture of goodwill on our part, there will be a delivery this afternoon of the green Burmese jade you asked for." He sat back and took a sip of the fruit juice that Jean had poured for him.

Miss Lim repacked the dress into the suit carrier and, zipping it up, nodded to Lee that it was time they were moving.

They stood up and shook hands all round. Jean showed them out to the lifts, and they said goodbye and left for the airport.

"Well, that was short and sweet," Barbara said as she dabbed around her face and neck with one of her small handkerchiefs.

"He never is one for drawing things out," replied Hector. "That's him all over. Once he sees something and verifies it, and Miss Lim runs her beady eye over it, it's all taken care of quickly and they move on to their next project. Jean, are you ready? Alex is waiting downstairs to drive you to the bank."

Jean clipped shut her compact and, taking the attaché case, went downstairs and climbed into the car.

Alex drove through the busy streets as quickly as he dared, which was a help to Jean. Her excitement had worn off a bit, and she now felt nervous and a bit sick, sat there with all that money in cash next to her. Normally, all of the Emporium's transactions were conducted by telegraphic transfer, so it was rare for her to have a large sum of cash in her hand, never mind that it was a couple of million.

The car arrived outside the bank and Alex held the door for Jean as she stepped out of the car. She scooted through the crowd of pedestrians like a football player dribbling the ball towards goal.

Inside the bank, Jean waited briefly while a clerk called to an office, and Mr Salleh came out to greet Jean and escort her into his office. She had known him for a number of years, so it relaxed her somewhat to know that the money would soon be safely deposited, and that he would hand her a receipt which she could then safely return to the Emporium.

He had been gone about ten minutes – no doubt, she thought, to count and deposit the money. Thank goodness she hadn't been made to queue up at the counter like everyone else. It wasn't the done thing to arrive at the head of the queue, only to announce that you wanted to bank two million dollars cash. This was by far a better approach, as well as being pleasantly cool too. She couldn't resist looking at the photos on Mr Salleh's desk, noting the two small faces of his children giggling at the camera.

Mr Salleh returned with a concerned look on his face and a couple of forms in his hand, which trembled ever so slightly. "Miss Cutting, I'm afraid there's a problem. It would seem that all the money you have brought in is counterfeit." The colour drained from her face as he continued: "We have enjoyed a long and well-founded relationship with the Barnes Oriental Gem Emporium. Indeed, you and I have known each other for some time now, so I hope I am right in assuming you knew nothing of this." His head inclined slightly as he looked directly at her, and waited for an answer.

"Oh, my goodness, no!" Jean exclaimed. "I – well, we – never thought this to be the case, since we received the money as payment in good faith. Oh my! The time – what's the time?"

He looked at the small clock on his desk. "It's a quarter to twelve."

Jean pulled herself together, and, making an effort to keep calm and controlled, made a plea to Mr Salleh. "Please hold the money for us until three o'clock before you do anything – I mean with the police and suchlike. I may just be able to rectify this, if time is on my side."

He took a moment to size up the lady in front of him. It was true that they had done business together for many years now, and therefore he knew that she was as straight as they came – hence his initial shock and dismay when discovering the money to be counterfeit. "I think, given the length of our association, that I can meet your request. But be back by three to clear things up. I shan't be able to control things in your favour any later than that."

Jean leapt to her feet and shook hands quickly. She dashed out of the office, across the main floor of the bank, and out to where Alex was quietly waiting to return her to the Emporium.

It was a surprise, given away by the expression on his usually non-committal face, for him to be told to take her to the airport – and fast. However, it was out of character for her to behave like this, so there must be a genuine need for him to respond.

So it was, with Alex speeding along the highway towards the airport, that Jean told him what had happened about the dress, the diamonds, the deal with Lee Eng Tek, and the fake money. Now their one chance was to reach Lee before he got his flight to Jeddah with the dress.

Alex had many contacts all over Singapore. You usually find that chauffeurs do. They chat with one another like a secret society, and, more often than not, know all of their boss's business, even when the boss doesn't think they do. Never underestimate a chauffeur; he will often have the key, or the resources, to solve many a problem.

Alex knew that Lee was going to Jeddah. Lee's driver had said so while they had a chat in the car park at the Emporium. He also knew that Miss Lim was flying up to Kuala Lumpur at around the same time as Lee's plane was departing. Since they were both flying Singapore Airlines, as Lee's driver had confirmed, it was easy to deposit both of them at the same entrance to the terminal at Changi.

Jean's stomach rolled at the very mention of the word deposit. She powdered her nose, and generally checked things over in the small mirror of her compact while Alex sped along. They would be certain to get a fine for this, but it seemed a small price to pay considering the alternative.

As if to remind them of the fine, a small chime kept going off, which meant that Alex had to slow down briefly for it to stop. This, thanks to the ingenuity of Singaporean society and law, was a device fitted to most vehicles driving in the republic, which alerted the driver to the fact that he had exceeded the speed limit. Therefore, there was never any question of doubt if fined, as the chime would give away the fact that the car had been speeding, and the driver would know about it the second he was over the limit.

Alex's chime was tinkling away like a baby's rattle in the shaking grip of said baby, yet this was getting to be rather exciting. Never before had either of them been in a situation where they were both prepared to break the law to put things right.

As Alex swung the car to a halt in front of the terminal, Jean jumped out and ran inside. As was the case for most of its operational hours, the terminal was busy. Queues of passengers snaked their way around signs and check-in counters.

Looking up at the screens, and the large digital-display departure board, Jean picked out the flight to Jeddah, which blinked back at her with the word 'closing' ominously lit in red. Running to a window near a fast-food outlet, she watched despairingly as, true to the prediction, she could see an air bridge pull away from the door of an aircraft, and a tug begin to push the plane back from its stand. It started its engines, winding up in tone to declare itself ready for departure.

"That's that, then," she muttered to herself, and, turning back, she began to walk towards the door of the terminal. As she excused her way through several queues, she remembered that Alex had said that Miss Lim was flying back to Kuala Lumpur. It was worth a look, so she scoured the boards for the next flight.

The services that operated between Singapore and Kuala Lumpur run on a regular shuttle basis, so there's always a departure available for the business commuter.

The next flight was due to leave at five to three, so Jean found where the check-in desk was for SQ112, and sat down a short distance away. She didn't have to wait long before Miss Lim appeared and checked in for the flight. As she turned round from the counter, there was Jean ready to pounce.

"I think before you leave our fair city that you and I need to have a little chat." Not giving Miss Lim the chance to question her, Jean linked arms and escorted her over to the seating area where she had been waiting. "I know that Lee's flight has departed. You probably did the same as me, and watched the plane go just to make sure. However, I also know that he trusts you with the running of his business in his absence, as Hector does me. So, before you go, perhaps you would accompany me to the branch of our bank here in the terminal, and we can set things right with a transfer of funds from your account into ours. Neat, no fuss, and legal, it's so unlike that last attempt to fleece us."

Miss Lim stared venomously at Jean. "I don't know what you're talking about; and as for handling me in this way, I shall make sure it is reported to Mr Lee when he returns from Saudi Arabia."

Jean rolled her eyes impatiently, and sighed. "Don't give me that routine, dear, you know me to be a worthy adversary, we are both prepared to fight to defend our employers, but this time your scheme has backfired. The bank confirmed, pretty quickly I should add, that all the money you brought to the Emporium was counterfeit. So, don't think you can pull wool over my eyes. Let's get along now to the bank branch, it's just here past the end row of check-in counters. After all, it won't take long, and I'm sure you don't want to miss your flight do you?"

Miss Lim looked at the times on the departures boards, and back at Jean. "He didn't think those other two would notice in time. They're not exactly in our league anyway."

Jean smarted. "Perhaps not, but as family, they are part of the Emporium, and therefore, are my responsibility. Besides, it was me who caught the announcement that the money was all fake when I went to the bank after you two had departed for the airport. I'm not prepared to answer charges for money laundering, fraud, or whatever else they would decide to throw at me, just because your boss deemed Barbara and Stuart as naive and unimportant pawns in his game. He's on his way to Jeddah, armed with a very valuable birthday present for a princess. She'll love it no doubt, and his client will end up paying probably more than two million for the pleasure of seeing a happy birthday girl."

By now they had arrived at the bank's airport branch on the main concourse of the terminal. As she wrote out details for the transfer of funds, Miss Lim permitted herself a small smile. "Actually we're getting three million for the dress. The family were delighted with Mr Lee's idea of the gift, and the stones are indeed beautiful. I doubt they'll ever see the outside world ever again – just small family gatherings in the desert."

Passing the details for the transfer across the counter to the bank teller, Jean interrupted, feeling it important to underscore her side of this transaction. "Mr Salleh at your Tanglin Road branch will be expecting this transfer of funds via the express clearing house system. I believe it can be confirmed and put through in no more than a couple of hours? Would you inform him I'll be back at his branch to conclude our business there."

The teller hopped off her chair, and half opened her mouth to say that a couple of hours was the minimum time for funds to go between branches of the bank. The look she got from Jean thwarted her speech, so she nodded, went to the rear of the office, made a call, worked for a few minutes on a computer, and returned with a stamped printout for Jean and a copy for Miss Lim, which she snatched, and stuffed into her briefcase.

"There, all done," smiled Jean sweetly. "Needs must when the devil drives, so I shan't detain you any longer, Miss Lim. You may wish to check out the cosmetics in the duty-free shops. You appear to be perspiring somewhat."

Making that her parting shot, she sailed outside and back into the car where Alex had been waiting for her.

"Back to the bank now please, Alex, I've got to pacify Mr Salleh before we return to the Emporium."

Shortly before three, Jean returned to Mr Salleh's office, where she presented her copy of the transfer receipt, and he made a call, confirming that all had worked out well. Relief visited Mr Salleh's face, and he looked at the counterfeit money that sat on the desk in front of him.

"You will, of course, understand that we must retain this money, it wouldn't do for it to be in the wrong hands."

"Oh, I quite agree," proclaimed Jean, "but seeing as this transfer mirrors our original intent, I hope that the Emporium's name won't be tarnished in any way. I'd imagine your superiors would be thrilled with you for foiling such a large sum's fall into your bank. I'm sure the information from the transfer at the airport will give you the details you need, should you ever have to take the matter further."

Mr Salleh and Jean shook hands, before she left the bank, and flopped into the back seat of the car .

Alex looked in the rear-view mirror. "Can we go home now?"

"Yes, I think we can," Jean said as she fumbled around in her handbag for her compact.

Walking back into Hector's office, Jean was greeted by three very worried people, who, in the time that she had been away, had covered about every possibility as to her whereabouts with all that money. Having made herself and Hector a cup of green tea, and having poured chilled juice for Barbara and Stuart, she sat them down and told them what had transpired.

"So in the end all's well. Here is the deposit slip, and Mr Salleh said it'll be in the account the day after tomorrow."

Barbara blew her nose loudly. "I knew that man wasn't to be trusted. I knew, didn't I, Stuart, that all was not quite genuine with him?"

Stuart leant back in his chair and exhaled dramatically. "Well, I guess we have Jean here to thank for the successful outcome of this whole saga with the frock. I'm just trying to picture a Saudi princess wearing a drag dress, all of a sparkle in the desert sun with sequins and diamonds! Candy would be thrilled to know his handiwork was being appreciated by royalty!"

More out of relief than anything, they all sat around the table and laughed heartily.

Jean decided that, after what she had just gone through, juice and green tea hadn't quite hit the mark, so, after pouring some good whisky into tumblers with ice, she passed the drinks around. Together they toasted Candy, the Saudi royal family, and (with the suggestion from Barbara) Bonnie, who would be getting some new toys and blankets when they got home.

Chapter Six

New Year – New Fortune

Part of the reason that Hector had wanted Barbara and Stuart to go to Singapore with him at that time, was that at the end of January the Chinese New Year celebrations would be taking place.

This only manifested itself in the minds of Barbara and Stuart when they were out shopping one day. Things had returned to normality after the cheque had cleared, and Mr Salleh had handed over credit cards and cheque books in the names of Barbara and Stuart. Since then, they had enjoyed several long shopping excursions. On this day, however, they couldn't fail to notice decorations being put up and small trees in pots being placed outside doors. There was a lot of red everywhere, prompting Stuart to wonder if they were really in Singapore, and not Peking.

They were having a break in between shops, and were sat by the statue of the merlion, which faced out into Marina Bay. A small group of tourists were being given a guided tour, and were being told about the merlion and its symbolic association with Singapore.

"I'm surprised it's not known to its friends as Raffles," chuckled Stuart.

Barbara thought it a nice image, and, when you thought about it, half fish and half lion was quite apt for Singapore. After all, they had traded here for centuries, and, shipping-wise, it was a major crossroads in Asia. Certainly, in recent years, the business dealings done in Singapore and by Singaporeans elsewhere had deserved the lion image. It seemed that if Hong Kong had the dragon, then it was only right that Singapore had the merlion.

Stuart sat transfixed by Barbara's monologue. "Where did all that come from? Have you been swallowing books?"

"Not really – " sniffed Barbara, "just reading the *Straits Times* every morning with Hector on the balcony, but that's hours before you get up, dear. I just want to keep abreast of things here now that it's the home to my money. There's no point in having all this wealth if you don't understand fully where it comes from." Shooting a sideways glance at him, Barbara felt she had made her point, so she got up and waddled off towards a metro station with several bags swinging from her shoulder.

Stuart half ran to catch up, and they took the metro across to what had become one of Barbara's favourite haunts – Bugis Street.

Pronounced boogie, Bugis Street had, at one time, been a seething mass of street traders. It had a more than dubious reputation after nightfall, since it was known to be packed with hookers of all fragrances and flavours.

Consequently, in recent years the Singapore government decided that this wasn't quite the image it wanted to project. Since a fine for wearing cheap scent and lipstick seemed somewhat inappropriate, they decided to bleach the street of any character that it had taken some years to accumulate, and to redress the street as somewhere that the tourist could spend many a happy hour shopping for CDs and local souvenirs. Fruit stalls were allowed, and the ambience of the street was therefore enhanced by the pungent smell of durian – an Asian fruit of great popularity. The locals enjoyed the fruit itself, as well as the spectator sport of watching German tourists sniffing it and pulling faces once a small piece had been popped into their mouths by a helpful and charming small child. Durian is known to the more well-heeled traveller as having such a strong odour that it conjures up mental images more associated with a farmyard silage drum or a goat's pen.

Barbara had no problem with farmyard associations, and had eaten quite a large portion of the fruit whilst she stood chatting with locals. Stuart, on the other hand, did not express any desire whatsoever to try durian, so he amused himself by haggling for some batik material at one of the stalls, gleefully making a lot of noise in the process.

It was after six by the time they both got back to Hector's apartment, where they found him sat on the balcony having a whisky with Jean.

At the same moment, Lee Eng Tek was pondering on the thought that he would have sold his soul for a shot of whisky. As it was, the party in Jeddah, despite being glaringly over the top in its style and presentation, was predictably devoid of alcohol.

It was to be expected after all, Lee decided with a small sigh, that one had to respect the culture and religion of one's clients. Sucking heavily on a chilled fresh mango juice, he picked up the call on his cellphone from Miss Lim.

A few minutes later, having listened to the strains of Miss Lim explaining what had happened at Changi with Jean, Lee switched his cellphone off and rejoined the party. The father of the party girl was busily ordering a camel race to take place within the hour under a night sky littered with fireworks.

The birthday girl herself sat demurely with her sisters and mother, gazing into the sky and clapping her hands with glee at the spectacle of so many fireworks. She managed to conceal her rampant excitement at the prospect of trying on the dress with the diamonds that would sparkle like the stars above.

Lee satisfied himself that here, at least, was a job well done. As for his next task, he would use these nights in the desert to put together a scheme which would remind Hector Barnes, once and for all, that it was he, Lee Eng Tek, who had the entire Orient at his fingertipped control. Switching his cellphone back on, he punched in some numbers and glanced at his watch. Despite the time difference, there would be no doubt that the receiver of his call would agree to help. A score had to be settled.

Jean typed furiously on her keyboard, setting up a contract for the Italians to sign in order to complete their deal with Hector.

This had been some time in the making, but now, finally, they had come to Singapore. Delight had filled their faces when they had seen the Burmese jade. Along with the premium-quality rubies and some rather good South African diamonds, the design for their new Tricolore range would be a roaring success back in Milan. Their bliss knew no bounds – at least, in the pure Italian sense.

Hector presented the freshly typed contract to Gianfranco Maggiore, who, on behalf of his company, signed the two pages required.

Jean deftly removed the signed contract and produced some freshly brewed espresso and grappa, which drew rapturous applause from the party sat around the conference table. Someone had a small camera, and photos were taken to commemorate the event.

Half an hour later, the Italians left Hector's office. Jean returned to Hector, smiling to herself like the proverbial cat that's had the cream. "That went well. I was pleased to see that they were as Italian as we hoped they would be, and not mono-European, like so much of Europe is today."

Hector passed her some paperwork. "Quite so. We can get moving on the export order now. Have you heard from Barbara or Stuart yet today?"

Jean looked at her watch. "They'll be having lunch at Newton Circus. I told them about the hawkers' food market there, so they've gone to try some kway teow. They're going to make their way here later so we can all go for dinner. Alex will take us at six to the Pan Pacific for drinks, and then on for dinner at the Sheraton Towers on Scotts Road."

"Excellent," beamed Hector, and he carried on working while Jean returned to her roost and put through a call to Hector from the opal company in Sydney.

Alex collected a pouch from her desk, and left for the afternoon's errand run around the city – a routine he was used to.

Miss Lim pressed hard with a teaspoon on the slice of lemon that was floating in her tea. She had been told to wait by Lee, and wait she would. She was happy to spin the time away, knowing that what would unfurl later would be deliciously exacted revenge for her and her employer.

At six o'clock, or, to be precise, according to Jean's watch, three minutes past, Barbara and Stuart exited the lift and stopped by Jean's desk for a chat. She was just arranging the cover over her keyboard and computer, and advised them that Hector would be finished shortly. She couldn't help but notice a more than usual amount of squirming and fidgeting going on between them, and asked if they were okay.

"We're fine, dear," giggled Barbara. "We've been shopping and we've bought you a gift – just a small something to say thanks for all your efforts on our behalf."

Jean twitched with excitement. "A gift? For me? You shouldn't have."

"Yeah, we know," smiled Stuart, "but we couldn't resist it." With that, he produced with a flourish a small box wrapped with some raw-silk ribbon. "Something for your mantelpiece."

Jean untied the ribbon and opening the box, pulled out a small wire tree. It had semi-precious stones stuck to it with fat gobs of glue in order to resemble fruit and leaves adorning the unknown type of tree. Jean thought it looked like the bonsai version of a twelve-year-old's metalwork project from a comprehensive school. It was hideous, but, seeing the radiance coming from Barbara's face, she pecked their cheeks and said in the true British manner, "It's lovely. I shall treasure it and think of you both every time I look at it."

Barbara was pleased. "You see, I told you she'd like it."

Hector emerged from his office, admired the tree, and shepherded them all into the lift and down to where Alex was stood waiting by the car.

Drinks were taken in the lounge of the Pan Pacific Hotel. Barbara and Stuart, who had both decided several days earlier to conduct a test and search out the best Singapore-sling cocktail, took note of the surroundings, the drink itself, the nibbles that were offered, and the general ambience of the lounge.

This entertained both Hector and Jean, who sat quietly amused by the spectacle of two tourists doing the 'we're in Singapore tonight, darling' scenario, oblivious to the world turning around them.

Barbara announced that, in her opinion, this was the best sling yet, and confirmed it by sucking the last drops of cocktail out of the small crevices in between some ice cubes with her well-trained straw.

On this cue, Hector stood. "I think we'll go for dinner now. There's a table booked for us at the Li Bai restaurant in the Sheraton Towers, and, though I say so myself, it is rather good."

Stuart clapped his hands in eager delight. "Sounds divine. C'mon then, let's go," and pulled Barbara out of her squidgy corner of the sofa.

Hector strode out of the main entrance, ahead of the chattering between Jean and Barbara, who were engrossed in discussing the pleasures to be gained from the fine art of fruit-carving. Jean had recently started an evening class, conducted by a small man from Thailand, and was relatively pleased with her initial work of a florally cut chunk of watermelon. Barbara wondered if the same principle might help liven up the dinner table back at the Bide-a-Wee if she hacked away at a pound of pears for long enough.

They stopped and looked around for Hector and Alex. Across the car park they watched open-mouthed as Alex, instead of opening the car door for Hector, neatly, and with strength, clubbed him on the back of the head. Alex pushed the crumpling body into the back of the car, before he scooted round to the driver's seat. In what seemed like a matter of seconds, he reversed the car and sped off into the busy evening traffic.

As Jean and Stuart began to run across the forecourt of the hotel, alarming the hotel staff with cries for help, all they could see was Hector's car melting into the traffic flow, before Alex took a side turn and disappeared into oblivion. Barbara stood rooted to the spot, and wailed like a banshee.

Some hours later Hector stirred. Not being able to stretch, he quickly realised that he was firmly tied up and gagged with a length of cloth, which was knotted in the middle. It seemed pointless to try to struggle free, at least for the time being, so he concentrated on adjusting his eyes to the dim light around him, trying to get an idea of where he was.

As his eyes grew accustomed to the light, despite the splitting headache and throbbing pain on the back of his head, he managed to raise his head slightly and take a look around. A few feet away he noticed, with a jump, that there was an elderly Chinese woman squatting on a small stool, rocking an infant to sleep in her arms. She looked at Hector and gave him her best effort of a broad grin. She possessed only one tooth, which hung, decaying, at a precarious angle in her gaping mouth.

There was music and singing in the background. Was he in a cinema? No, that wasn't it. A theatre perhaps? There was the strong odour of grease and make-up. Creaking floorboards made it difficult to move without attracting attention, but he could see some scenery leaning against a wall opposite him. He could also hear traffic in the distance and smell cooking, so it dawned on him that in fact he was outdoors.

A curtain was pulled back and someone leaned over to have a good look at him. The face that met his was made up in the style of Chinese opera – an art form that, over the thousands of years of its history, has gained heavyweight respect for all who choose to take it as their profession. The art of applying correct make-up for the myriad of character roles takes a long time to learn in itself, as Hector appreciated whilst he stared face-to-face with his captor.

The man grunted, stood up, and scolded the old woman. The brightly coloured costume swished as the man left through the same curtain partition, and the old woman placed the now sleeping infant into a wooden crib, where it started snoring gently.

The old woman lifted the lid off a bubbling pot, and, as the steam filled her face, she made self-congratulatory noises to herself, along the lines that even at her age she could still manage to produce good food. Carrying a ladle full of the hot broth across to Hector, she rested on her haunches while he sipped it from her. Then she returned to the pot, swinging the ladle triumphantly in the knowledge that someone at least appreciated her cooking. Hector hadn't been able to pinpoint the flavour, but felt that he should drink it all, for there was no knowing when next he would get something to eat.

The music stopped and the cast appeared back through the curtain. Stepping over and around him, they changed out of their costumes in the manner of 'eager to be somewhere else at this time of night'. The infant's mother checked her sleeping angel, whispered something to the old woman, and, for the first time, several of the cast looked over their shoulders and stared at Hector.

At this point, Alex appeared and dispatched them all with a few well-chosen words. Not wanting to argue, they left, leaving Alex standing over Hector with his head slightly cocked while he sized the situation up.

Minutes later, Hector felt himself being rolled up in an oily thick sheet, and, with the help of an unknown person, he was carried down some steps from the shanty theatre and laid in the boot of his car. They drove for some time before coming to a stop. When he was unfurled from the stinking sheet, he found himself lying at the fashionably chic feet of Miss Lim.

"*Kong Hay Fat Choy*," she purred at him.

"Happy New Year to you, too," he replied, before laying the side of his face back down on the cold marble floor.

Jean had taken Barbara and Stuart back to Hector's apartment, where they now sat, trying to think of what to do next.

"We ought to call the police and report a kidnapping," barked Stuart.

"Normally I'd agree with you, but I've a nasty feeling whom the guilty party is. For the next few hours at least, we should sit tight and wait for contact to be made, for I'm certain that it will be."

Jean was convincing, and, between the three of them, they agreed to wait a while.

Jean's prediction came true when, a couple of hours later, the telephone rang. Feeling that Barbara was too much of a snivelling mess to speak, and Stuart too much on the jagged edge of hysteria, she removed a pearl earring and lifted the receiver. "Mr Barnes' apartment. How may I help?" she said calmly. It sounded absurd, even to her, to answer the phone in this way, yet right from the start Jean decided that things should be conducted properly; it might save any messy business later on.

Miss Lim was brief but clear. "Miss Cutting, we are interested in an exchange. Please be so good as to draw up one of your fine contracts for the transfer of the Barnes Oriental Gem Emporium into the control of Mr Lee Eng Tek. You have until eleven o'clock in the morning to do this. Wait at your office for further instructions. If you do as I ask, then you shall receive Mr Barnes back unharmed – or, at least, in one piece, which by our standards is rare."

The line went dead and Jean sighed, brushing a hand over her tired brow. Turning away from the phone, she faced Barbara and Stuart, who were tightly packed together on a sofa, both looking at her with eyes imploring for good news. She told them what had been dictated to her by the poisonous Miss Lim, and they sat huddled together round a bottle of whisky while the hours ticked by and a plan hatched itself.

"Well, I must say his timing is impeccable," Jean conceded. "Tomorrow night is the Chinese New Year festival, not only here in Singapore but all over Asia. There will be thousands out and about celebrating, and a lot of fireworks and crackers. In other words, plenty of noise to deafen our ears to some more sinister noises."

Barbara's eyes welled up again. "Oh, don't say that. You make it sound like we'll never see him again, and we've only just got to know him – well, as family. He's one of our own now." On that note, she removed one of her small handkerchiefs and blew her nose severely.

Stuart got up and paced around the lounge, out onto the balcony and back inside again. "It's precisely because he is one of our own now that we have to do something."

Jean raised her eyebrows and sighed. "I agree sincerely, but what exactly?"

Although appearing to be restless and irritable, Stuart's mind was clear and racing away with an idea. "Jean, do as the bitch says and draw up a contract. We'll go to the office in the morning, together, just in case there are eyes everywhere watching our every move. Right now, though, Jean, you should go home. You look like you could do with a rest in your own domain."

Putting his arm around her shoulders, Stuart escorted Jean out of the lounge and into the hallway, whispering some instructions that brought a blush to her cheeks and a hand to her mouth. Despite the initially muttered protests, she shrugged her shoulders, nodded in agreement, and left.

Back in the lounge, Barbara lit a cigarette and, curling one leg up onto the sofa, looked into the twinkling eyes of her son and said, not for the first time, "What are you up to, my lad?"

At ten the next morning, Barbara and Stuart took a taxi to the Emporium, where they found Jean hunched over her desk reading her freshly typed and printed efforts, and cuddling a small Chinese teacup with some green tea steaming in it.

"How are we doing?" Stuart asked, with the smallest of smiles creeping across his face.

Jean produced an overnight bag from under her desk. "It may not be what you're used to, but it was the best I could muster at short notice."

"Bravo!" declared Stuart and, taking the other bag that Barbara had brought with her, he disappeared into the men's toilet along the corridor.

Jean looked at Barbara. "Are you sure this is the right thing to do? Will it work? After all, if it doesn't, the price to pay will be too much to contemplate."

She took out her compact and powdered her face busily as Barbara looked out of the window.

"He really is very good, and I have total trust in him. If anyone can do it, he can." She turned and perched on the corner of Jean's desk, folding her hands on her lap. "Provided we follow the instructions set out, it will all be fine. Just don't forget to make the call at the right time."

Jean clipped shut her compact. "I shan't. I promise. We have to be a team on this. Some green tea perhaps?"

Barbara's face contorted. "Oh God, no! Just some coffee, if there's any going."

They occupied themselves in the small kitchen, both agreeing that it was best to keep their hands busy; and presently a large pot of coffee was carried into Hector's office. They both sat around his desk, taking comfort in the surroundings, which defined the man that they were going to save and the business which he so passionately believed in.

At eleven o'clock on the dot the phone rang, making them both jump. Jean answered the call, deciding that for the time being it was most certainly, "The Barnes Oriental Gem Emporium. Good morning."

Miss Lim didn't want to waste time with pleasantries. Lee Eng Tek was sat in a shadowy corner, which suited his demeanour perfectly. He was watching the proceedings with extreme attention to detail, and Miss Lim was acutely aware of his focus on her every move and breath. It had seemed appropriate to bring Hector into the room for the start of their day's work. Although still tied and gagged, he was propped into an ornate Chinese high-backed chair, which, owing to the lack of arm rests, meant that he had to concentrate on keeping his balance. He listened intently while Miss Lim made her play, and with a flick of her hair she gave her instructions to Jean.

Jean, holding the phone just far enough away from her ear so that both she and Barbara could hear what was said, made the right punctuation noises, and only when Miss Lim paused did Jean interject. "Well, actually, it won't be myself to attend. You may think you know all our affairs, but that's not entirely so. We have a sleeping partner, based in Australia. She's arriving later this afternoon. It will be her that you will have to meet."

Miss Lim knitted her brow, and, putting her hand over the receiver, she told Lee about the Australian connection. He sat forward and spoke quietly to Hector. "You never mentioned this before, not in all the years we have been trading together. We know you hold offshore accounts, and deal regularly with both suppliers and clients in Australia, but do you really have a sleeping partner dozing away in there?"

Hector raised his head slowly and looked at Lee with utter contempt. Breathing heavily, he made noises to speak. Lee motioned to one of his henchmen, who stepped forward out of the dark corners of the room and loosened the gag, allowing Hector to drink in several gasps of air. "Yes, a sleeping partner, just for a rainy day's sake."

With that, the gag was replaced and Lee sat back in his chair, waving Miss Lim to continue, nodding that it would do.

"We don't care who is there, so long as they have the contract with them, and no police hidden away. Any trouble and you'll have to fish your precious Mr Barnes out of Marina Bay."

Jean's hand trembled as, for the first time in many years, she made charade-like gestures to Barbara, who obliged and passed her a freshly lit cigarette. "We understand entirely. What time and where shall the exchange take place?"

"Eight o'clock this evening, on Boat Quay. Precisely where will be told to you at six. Until then, Miss Cutting, stay by the phone." The line went dead and Miss Lim replaced the receiver, permitting herself a smile towards Lee.

Jean and Barbara sat puffing away on their cigarettes like a pair of trench soldiers about to go over the top.

As they stubbed their cigarettes out, the door to Hector's office flew open and a heavily made-up middle-aged woman grinned at them before walking into the middle of the room and treating them to a twirl. A ripe Australian accent barked, "Where the hell's my baggage? I've just landed from Oz, an' there's not a pair of knickers in sight! By the way, let's do the formalities first. I'm Bonnie – Bonnie Chalmers – from Sydney 'Stralia, per-leased to meetcha, girls."

Jean looked at Barbara. "It might just work. Give me another ciggie, dear."

Stuart stood proudly on the spot whilst Barbara and Jean fussed around him, tucking here, pulling there, and, with a final touch from Jean's compact, the image was complete.

An hour later Stuart took a taxi out to Changi. Looking at the arrivals board and seeing that a flight had just arrived from Sydney, he pulled his bag on wheels into the toilets, and changed.

Bonnie Chalmers emerged from the crowded arrivals hall, and, loudly protesting at having been landed in Singapore without baggage, she swore enough to draw attention to herself. She flung herself into the back of a taxi, announcing loudly that she had to be "At the Barnes Oriental Gem Emporium urgently – so get a bloody move on, will ya?"

A car joined the snaking line of traffic out of the airport and, keeping its distance, followed the taxi all the way into the city. It's occupants observed Bonnie struggle out of the taxi, swear at the driver, who'd never heard language like it from a lady, and stomp inside the main entrance of the Emporium. A call was made on a mobile phone from the watching car, and, nodding, the driver switched off the engine and waited to follow the next move and the instructions that accompanied it.

Bonnie ran from the lift and collapsed on the sofa in Hector's office. "It's such an old trick, but it worked. I powdered my nose nearly the whole way, off and on, and saw in the compact's mirror a car tail me from Changi. It had to be Lee's men. They're outside here now, waiting for us to leave for Boat Quay."

Jean kissed the heavily powdered cheek. "Stage one – check. Good and well done. But let's not get carried away – after all, dear, you're a brash Australian businesswoman, not an Aussie drag queen."

Bonnie agreed, lighting a cigarette and thinking how thrilled Dale would be if he could see her now.

Jean replaced the telephone receiver with a sigh. "We can only hope that our connections at the embassy will be able to pull a string or two for us."

Barbara raised an eyebrow. "Can we? What embassy?"

Jean reached for her compact, but remembered instantly that Stuart had it. So, holding her hand out in his direction, she elaborated: "Well, at least one thing's gone right for us. With it being the New Year, His Excellency the Ambassador is having a party on his yacht this evening – Drinks, nibbles, music, and a slow cruise for the evening around the bay. After all, it's probably the best vantage point for seeing the festivities."

Barbara and Stuart looked at each other blankly.

Jean began to get impatient. "I've just secured some impromptu invitations to the party. We'll be joining the yacht later."

With that, they talked over their plans for the evening while Stuart removed his wig and had a good scratch.

Jean never had thought of Miss Lim as tardy, so it was no surprise to her that at six o'clock precisely the phone on Hector's desk rang. She lifted the receiver and listened intently, jotting down notes on a pad.

After the call, she phoned for a taxi, and, making sure she had all she needed in her handbag, signalled to Barbara that they should leave. "Come along, dear, we need to go. The Ambassador's party is about to cast off. Stuart, are you sure you can handle this. I'm only going to ask the once. If you're not happy, we'll call the whole thing off and play it straight."

Stuart pulled his wig back on. "Play it straight? Like hell! Now get along, you two, Bonnie's gotta get her Aussie brain into gear."

Taking the jotted notes from Jean, he hugged Barbara and Jean and the two ladies departed.

He stood in the dark, looking out of the office window down to the busy streets below. It seemed as if rush hour was going in one direction and New Year party revellers were streaming in the other. It was all somewhat different from a New Year at home. Despite liking Singapore, something he had never had any doubt about, Stuart missed home, the J & J, the gang and a small pug.

'Still, get this lot sorted, have a big bash to celebrate, and then go home with Mum to plan for the future, thanks to the sale of Dad's diamonds.'

It seemed odd, but, for the first time, the thought crossed Stuart's mind that in actual fact the tea caddy had been left to Hector, and, as such, had the diamonds been too? It seemed hopeful to surmise that his dad had planned things to happen this way. Knowing that Hector was so stiff and morally correct about everything, he had had no reason to think of Hector acting any other way than he had done. Nevertheless, those diamonds had brought them closer together, although this was turning into an adventure that he hadn't anticipated. Stuart decided that, when all was said and done, with or without the diamonds, there was one commodity that remained above all else priceless in this modern world, and that was the sense of family and the feeling of belonging that everyone seeks.

Shaking himself out of his daydream, he looked at his reflection in the window, growled, and walked out of Hector's office. Picking up a handbag from Jean's desk, he entered the lift, and, as the doors closed, an Australian accent could be heard to declare, "Okay, you bahst'ds, time for tonight's show."

Chapter Seven

A Slow Boat to Sentosa

Hector could smell incense. His senses could sense incense – not something easily said by someone with a lisp, which is what made him laugh to himself. One of Lee's thugs rolled him over and asked what he was laughing at. The fact that the man actually had a lisp didn't help matters, and before long Hector was going red in the face with convulsive laughter. The thug removed the gag. It wouldn't do for the man to be dead from hysterical laughter and choking before he had served his purpose.

Miss Lim stepped through a beaded curtain and looked from Hector to the thug and back again. She tutted to herself, cursed the thug, and returned to her place beside Lee Eng Tek.

He clipped shut his mobile phone and quietly gave orders to a couple of men stood in front of him. They left, and he smiled at Miss Lim. "I'm not malicious by nature, but I've decided that once and for all the East belongs to me, and is not to be shared with him."

Miss Lim fizzed with excitement inside. Soon she would be able to oust that ridiculous woman, and make her own empire in the shadow of her master.

Hector felt himself being blindfolded, before being taken outdoors to the rear of a car. Amid the strong mixed smell of Tiger balm and Chanel, he was driven around the back streets of the city. Sounds coming from shopfronts reached him, and the smell of the hawkers, busy cooking their own brand of fast food, reminded him of how hungry he was. With all the turns that the car was taking, he was sure it was Alex driving. How could he have been so wrong about his driver? After all, he always classed himself as a good judge of character. Everyone has a price, so it had become apparent with Alex – a pity.

The car stopped, and he was taken hurriedly into the back entrance of a building and dumped unceremoniously in the corner of a hot and sweaty room.

The building itself fronted onto Boat Quay, right in the centre of the city. For many years it was the major place for trading deals to take place, and for the loading and unloading of various cargos. It still retained the original building facades, complete with shuttered windows, and had become a popular spot for people to eat out at, thanks to the many restaurants and food stalls located along the quayside next to the Singapore river. Tonight it was particularly busy with diners, and groups of tourists dawdling along the quay in search of culinary challenges.

Lee peeked through the shutters of an upstairs window and spotted a taxi pulling up. From the rear of the taxi, he was surprised to see a middle-aged woman climb out and swear loudly at the driver for what she seemed to believe had been an overpriced journey.

A call to his mobile earlier had confirmed that she had left the Barnes Gem Emporium, and she had been tailed for the trip to Boat Quay. There had been no interruptions to the ride, and she had not spoken to anyone except the poor driver, for whom Lee felt a brief pang of compassion.

"She's here and waiting where we told her to, next to the Makan Time sign downstairs. Take our guest down to her, and get that contract. Make sure he signs it before you hand him over."

Receiving her commands, obediently Miss Lim left Lee's side, and, with two thugs to pick up Hector, they made their way down onto street level.

Bonnie Chalmers had never liked Asia. It was enough that the Japanese had taken the chance to develop parts of Queensland, converting resorts into Japanese-friendly honeymoon destinations for the plane-loads that arrived weekly from Tokyo. All right, it had brought a lot of money into the Australian economy, but, she felt, now was the time for Australian business entrepreneurs, such as herself, to take a lead role and send the Japanese businessmen packing back to where they came from.

She was expanding nicely on this theory, thanks to a couple of memories of chats with Dale at the J & J, and several tourists had stopped to join in the debate. Then, as she removed her smoky sunglasses and breathed on them before giving them a quick polish with her scarf, she spotted Miss Lim and Hector, accompanied by what could only be called the oriental equivalent of two Sly Stallones.

She broke off from the group now around her, and walked towards Miss Lim. This was going to be hard. Although they had only met once, Stuart knew her to be as sharp as a knife.

So, taking a deep breath, Bonnie exclaimed, "Strewth, Hector, you look tirrible – shite, in fact. Best you come home with me. You could do with a break. C'mon back to Oz for a week or two. Bonnie'll getcher pecker goin' again."

Miss Lim only had one thing on her mind – the contract. "Did you bring the paperwork? Without it we keep him, and he'll end up as food for your precious Australian sharks."

"Oh, don't choo worry 'bout that. He's more important to me than yer stoopid contract. Yeah, I've brought it. Here ya go."

With that, Bonnie opened the handbag and produced the folded contract which Jean had typed earlier. Miss Lim was beside herself, sure in the fact that Lee would be pleased with her. However, there were a lot of people about who were taking second looks, so better get it over with.

"Okay, you sign it first and then you can go."

Hector raised his head, squinting in the light from the quayside and the general buzz that prevailed. "I'm not signing anything. Screw you!" gurgled out of his mouth.

Bonnie half laughed. "Ahh, c'mon, mate. Just sign the bloody thing. Do it for yer Bonnie."

Hector looked aghast at Bonnie, and, taking Miss Lim's pen, scrawled his signature on the dotted line indicated by her French-varnished fingernail.

Eager to get back to Lee with the contract, Miss Lim and her thugs dropped Hector into Bonnie's arms and retreated quickly back inside the building.

"Right," said Stuart, "let's go to a party."

Hector, who had continuously been staring at the apparition in front of him, found himself wondering if everyone around him had taken leave of their brain cells. "A party? Have you finally gone barmy? I've just signed away my life's work, and you want to party?" He was beginning to draw looks from passers-by.

As Bonnie steered Hector through the mingling crowd along the quayside, a mobile phone trilled for some attention with its own electronic version of 'Rule Britannia'.

Hector looked at Bonnie. "I think it's time for Stuart to come back, isn't it? And who's calling you at this moment in time?"

Bonnie stood on the edge of the quayside taking in the surroundings and the brewing celebrations. "Can't you tell by the ringtone? That'll be Jean – punctual, of course." Flicking the phone open, he announced loudly, to get above the general noise around him, "Yes, darling, we're here, where you said, so get that thing along pronto, will you?"

As they stood there, Hector sighted the bow of a large and well-lit yacht coming round a bend in the river, heading their way.

Back in the front room overlooking the quay, upstairs from Makan Time, Miss Lim presented the contract to Lee with the same reverence as a gun dog lays a dead pheasant at the feet of its master.

He unfolded it and quietly read it, noting Hector's signature at the bottom of it. After a moment, his face clouded over and blood rushed to his cheeks. "Did you read this contract before bringing it to me?" he asked, fixing Miss Lim with a concentrated stare.

She flicked her hair and played with the jade bracelet on her wrist. "Of course, and I made sure he signed it before letting him go."

"Well, then," hissed Lee, "you'll have noticed that what you've given me is not a contract for the transfer of the Barnes Oriental Gem Emporium into my power, but instead I've been given a ten-thousand-Singapore-dollar annual donation to the Singapore Botanical Society."

He sighed and looked out of the window just in time to see Bonnie removing her wig, thereby revealing Stuart, who had an itch on the back of his head. Following the direction of Stuart's gaze, he could see a yacht approaching the quayside with a party in full flow on the rear deck.

"If I can't have his company this way, we'll have to use other methods." Cocking his head towards his henchmen, who had momentarily distanced themselves from Miss Lim's side, he ordered, matter-of-factly, "Kill him – now. You've got a clear sight from this window."

A thug produced an automatic from his shoulder holster and aimed it through the shutters.

Jean was leaning on the bow railings of the yacht, named *Fiona* after the Ambassador's secretary. Waving her arms above her head in case they shouldn't see her, she called out, "Britannia's arrived to the rescue. Get ready to jump on deck. We're coming alongside shortly."

Hector was surprised to see Jean looking so liberated and free-spirited. She looked like one of those old-fashioned figureheads on the front of a galleon or tea clipper. The image suited her, and he felt a warm glow inside his chest as he realised how pleased she was to see him stood there with Stuart.

The yacht inched its way alongside the quay, and a deckhand held up an arm to guide Hector and Stuart towards the landing spot.

"Ready? On three we jump. One, two . . . "

As they jumped a single shot cracked through the air over the quayside. People looked round, keen to see firecrackers splinter themselves silly on the sidewalk.

All at once it dawned on someone that it hadn't been a firecracker at all, and they screamed, starting a wave of panic through the crowd along the quay.

On the deck, people had gathered round the two late arrivals to the party. Hector found himself looking at feet again, only this time they were patent-leather men's shoes, shiny and squeaky, and stood neatly together a few inches from the end of his nose. He stood up, aided by the deckhand, and shook hands with His Excellency, Sir Daniel Carstairs, Her Britannic Majesty's Ambassador to Singapore.

"Slightly unorthodox for an arrival on board *Fiona*, but you're very welcome," smiled Sir Daniel as he passed a sparkling champagne flute to Hector. "Perhaps you'd care to go below. There's a shower, and a dinner jacket for you pressed and ready."

Hector nodded in thanks. "That sounds like heaven. Shall we go, Stuart? I think Bonnie's fling in Singapore is over now, don't you?" He turned to beckon Stuart.

Stuart lay on the deck, motionless. The wife of one of the members of the Singapore Chamber of Commerce, who had been invited to the party, pushed her way through the group, pulling Barbara by the hand. The Ambassador called out for a doctor; surely Fiona had included one on the guest list.

Barbara fell to her knees next to Stuart, and placed her hand on his chest. Sticky with blood from an exit wound, she kept her hand on the spot to try to stem the flow, and, with her other hand, she did what a million other mothers have done to their children over the years. She spat into a small handkerchief and began wiping her son's face, cleaning it and, in this case, smearing make-up downwards to his neck. "Not my lovely boy. Please don't die and leave me. Not here, not now." A sob choked its way from the back of her throat, and she wished that she hadn't had that last glass of champagne.

Jean directed a doctor through the small crowd to Stuart's side. He assessed the scene, looking up at the Ambassador as he spoke. Sir Daniel nodded and, turning to an aide, ordered the yacht to pull in at the closest possible point.

As it happened, this was next to where the merlion statue stood to attention guarding the city, a steady jet of water streaming from its mouth. An ambulance was waiting on the quayside, so, with help from the deckhands, the doctor and Hector, they carried Stuart ashore. Amid the wailing of sirens, he was rushed to the hospital as fireworks blossomed in the night sky overhead.

Barbara sat in the hospital corridor, noting how bleached and sterilised it looked. She leaned her tired and weary head on Jean's shoulder and cried quietly for a few minutes.

Hector appeared, and sat down next to them. "Any news yet?"
Jean shook her head and asked where he'd been.

"The police were interested to hear my tale, and are now in haste to try and find Lee, or at the very least, Miss Lim – hopefully, before they can escape to another country. You know how quickly they can relocate."

A surgeon arrived at their side and, removing his mask, told them that Stuart had pulled through. "A couple of centimetres either side, and the result would have been very different. He's lost a lot of blood, but in time he'll make a full recovery. We're just settling him into a bed, and you can go and see him."

Barbara jumped to her feet and hugged the surgeon. "Thank you," she whispered, not only to the surgeon but, for the first time in a long while, to God for listening to her.

They were led into a room by a small Filipino nurse, who commanded that they remain only a short while since the patient had to rest.

They sat around Stuart. As he opened his eyes, blearily looking at his surroundings, he remarked, "This isn't the lounge deck of *Fiona*, is it? What happened?"

"A parting gift from Lee Eng Tek – meant for me, though, I think," answered Hector. "You're going to be fine, but rest is essential now."

Stuart looked at the three faces around him. "My family, all together, and here with me."

A tear streaked out of the corner of his eye, and Jean leant forward to wipe it away. "You see, we did it – a good team effort all round, I think." Stuart raised a weak smile. "Well, of course, with Bonnie Chalmers from Sydney it was bound to work. I guess the doctors worked all night but couldn't save your dress!"

They all laughed and, with Stuart in the middle, they linked hands, united to the core, signifying the essence of family, which they had all longed for in their own special ways.

Ten days later Stuart was assessed well enough to be discharged from the hospital. A flurry of nurses waved him off, for they had never had anyone quite like him to care for before. They had been entertained non-stop by his material and tantrums whilst he had been on their patch.

Hector and Barbara took him back to the apartment, and, for a couple of days, he lay on the chaise longue on Hector's balcony, calling for attention every few minutes.

Barbara smiled to herself, knowing that this was as sure a sign as any that her boy was mending nicely.

She sat on a stool next to him one afternoon, filing what was left of her fingernails and throwing out crossword clues, which Stuart had to keep scribbling out. "I think it's time we went home. Would you feel comfortable about going at the end of the week?"

Stuart turned onto his side, facing her, and put down the now shredded page of the newspaper. "Well, dear one, I think we've sensationalised this place for long enough. The vicar and his wife must now be up to their necks with pug poo in their garden, and I can almost hear Dale calling from behind the bar that drinks are on the house for us. The end of the week will do me just fine."

Barbara called Jean and asked her to book their flight home.

Hector got home around seven that evening. He confirmed that Jean had spoken to the airline, and that seats were booked for the Sunday night flight to Heathrow. "Get ready to go out for dinner. Jean's got a surprise for you both."

Stuart, at the mention of the word 'surprise', was showered, dressed and perfumed in twenty minutes. "So long as we don't have to go too far, it sounds like fun. *J'adore* surprises."

They found themselves back at the merlion, with Barbara and Stuart both looking round for signs of restaurants and food.

"Where's Jean, then?" asked Barbara. "She'll miss dinner, won't she?"

"Hardly – " said Hector, "here she comes now."

With that, they saw *Fiona* pull alongside with Jean stood on deck holding a champagne bottle in her hand, beckoning them aboard.

"With Sir Daniel's compliments," she grinned. "He felt that we should have a full evening with dinner on *Fiona* to compensate for the last time we were here. So climb aboard and the crew will take us to Sentosa and back."

Having eaten an excellent dinner, Barbara and Stuart were at the bow of the yacht, pointing out various sights of the Singapore cityscape by night. Hector joined Jean on the rear deck, passing her a glass of champagne with a smile. They sat quietly, watching Barbara and Stuart having fun.

Hector took a sip from the champagne and coughed slightly. "Could I interest you, perhaps, in dinner out tomorrow night, just the two of us?"

Jean looked at him, and then down at the ring on her finger. "Maybe if you rephrased it in a less formal manner, I might consider it."

Hector squirmed and, uncrossing his legs, rested his elbows on his knees. "I'm not terribly good at all this. It's been a long time since my last journey into the dating game. However, Jean, I would dearly love to spend an evening with you. So please would you consider it?"

Jean noticed his hunched figure leaning forward, looking almost sad, but not quite. He was perhaps just a little nervous, but not sad. It humbled her to see this big businessman behaving like a nervous teenager before her, and in her favour too. A sea breeze blew through her hair, and she herself realised that at this moment she too felt like a teenager. "I'd love to have dinner with you tomorrow night," she smiled. Too many years had passed since that New Year's Eve dance in Rangoon, and it was about time to let down her defences and reacquaint herself with some hitherto deeply buried feelings.

Barbara warmed to the touch of Stuart's arm around her shoulders. Since the shooting, she had blessed every minute with him, and she loved having her son's arm around her; it made her feel so safe.

Looking over her shoulder to the rear deck, and back again to Stuart, she asked, "Do you think he's made his move yet? It's about time those two dumped their hang-ups and got together. They're made for each other."

Stuart took a photo of the city, and had a swig of his champagne. "I agree entirely. This is the perfect spot and time for him to say something to her. I think he has realised that there's more to life than the Gem Emporium. Hopefully, she'll acknowledge that as well. Let's go and get some dessert. We can bring theirs out to them in a minute."

The yacht sailed gracefully across Marina Bay, along the shoreline of Sentosa and back to the city, where it docked just after midnight.

"Do thank Sir Daniel for us, won't you?" Barbara said as Jean left them to go home. "It was a lovely evening, and the dinner was delicious. The city looks so pretty at night with all its lights."

Jean climbed into a taxi and, looking out of the window, said, "I shall thank him on your behalf with pleasure. He's a good man and an excellent representative here for the UK. Hector, I'll see you tomorrow."

Hector shuffled briefly before stepping forward and pecking Jean goodnight on the cheek.

Barbara's arm nudged Stuart, and they nodded to each other, satisfied that the evening aboard *Fiona* had worked its magic for Hector and Jean, as well as giving them a special memory to keep for ever.

Chapter Eight

Dinner For Two

Raffles Hotel was declared open for business in 1887 by four brothers who were originally from Armenia. Following on from its humble beginnings as a colonial beach house, the hotel was developed, and named after Sir Thomas Stamford Raffles, the founder of modern Singapore. Growing in reputation over the years, it acquired a worldwide standard, and is known everywhere for the timeless elegance that it exudes. In 1987, the hotel's centenary year, it was created a national monument. The Republic of Singapore acknowledges the fact that the hotel forms a leading role in its tourism promotion all over the world, and the high standards associated with the hotel are maintained with a sense of pride by all who are involved with Raffles.

A table had been booked in the name of Barnes for dinner at eight. Hector ushered Jean through the main entrance of the hotel, and they spent a while browsing around the shops in the Palm Court before going to the Writer's Bar for drinks before dinner.

Soft piano music added ambience to the bar, known and previously frequented over the years by such greats as Coward, Kipling and Maugham.

Jean settled comfortably into her chair as Hector ordered cocktails. They chatted politely at first about general matters of the day and Barbara's efforts to try and secure a durian to take back to England. Despite Stuart's very vocal protest about the fruit, and its probable effects on the interior of the Bide-a-Wee, Barbara was determined to have a go.

After drinks, Hector escorted Jean into the Raffles Grill, where they were seated at their table smoothly and discreetly by the head waiter. Large chandeliers hung from the high ceiling, reminding diners of the elegant surroundings they were in. The restaurant hummed with quiet conversation. Menus were inspected, and both Hector and Jean relaxed into the mood of the restaurant, enjoying the perfectly cooked dinner which was placed before them.

"So, then, it's been a while since you brought anyone out for dinner?" Jean asked as she licked some raspberry coulis delicately off her spoon, and eyed her dinner partner with a subtle yet keen interest.

Hector was playing his game carefully. He had no intention whatsoever of making a complete hash of things, especially since it was Jean's pretty face that was opposite him. "Well, yes, I suppose it has. At least, it's been a while since I've had such charming company for dinner all to myself."

Jean's cheeks flushed the same colour as her raspberry coulis, and she set down her spoon, taking a sip of wine. "Well, between us I think there is more similarity than we'd perhaps both care to admit to. My usual evenings are easy-to-cook stir-fry meals for one, or, if I'm in the mood, something stodgy and English. Then it's on with a bit of fruit-carving (I like to think I'm getting quite good at it now), and then some tea before bed."

Hector smiled. "I'd have to concur that it's a pretty familiar picture you're painting, Jean, except mine is without the fruit-carving. A hobby is always a good thing to have for one's own time. It's just that I never seem to have the time on my hands to find a hobby, let alone pursue one."

Jean returned his smile. "Surely it's only now you notice that sort of thing – though, after all, it's years that you've lived here, and, as far as I know, nearly all your time has been spent working on the Gem Emporium."

Hector wiped his lips with his napkin. "It's been a very humbling thing to discover Barbara and Stuart. They're real people, who live hard and real lives. What you see is what you get – well, in Barbara's case anyway!"

They both giggled.

"Stuart is a bit more complex, though I've now learnt that it doesn't make him any less a person or character."

Jean stirred her coffee slowly, almost transfixed by the motion of stirring the small spoon clockwise, then anticlockwise, until satisfied.

Hector licked a finger and dabbed around the tablecloth, picking up a few crumbs along the route.

Jean smiled at him. 'Such an old-fashioned traditional gentleman,' she thought to herself.

As if to prove the words running through her mind, he paused mid-dab and expanded for her benefit. "During the war, we went to great lengths not to waste a single morsel, or crumb even.

116

Consequently, we were shown how to get the last crumbs up by licking our forefinger and dabbing around the tabletop. It's one of those habits that have never faded, and sometimes helps give me a childhood memory. It's funny how things can associate such sentimentality with the most simple of actions, isn't it?"

Jean nodded thoughtfully. She knew exactly what he meant. It was like rolling your thumbs around and around each other whilst your hands were folded. It had been something a young Jean had been hypnotised watching: her grandmother's hands folded neatly in the apron of her lap, and the thumbs rolling over and over whilst a story was told to the small child warming herself in front of an open fire. Great comfort was drawn from the strength of a loved one to watch over her, and at that very moment at a table in the Raffles Grill both Hector and Jean had the same idea dawn on them simultaneously. When all was said and done, the fondness, humour, comfort and strength, which they shared with each other, and had done for so long, was, in fact, another way of spelling that four-letter word with so many definitions – love.

Hector sighed. "Have we let so many years pass by refusing to acknowledge these feelings, and settling for something downgraded from the real, raw intensity of the pure emotion? If so, what are we left with? Is it too late for us?"

A brief spot of panic shot through his voice, and Jean placed a hand over the top of his hand, which, tired out from dabbing crumbs, now rested on the table.

"You can never say it's too late. We may have, over the years that we've known each other, allowed the emotions to dull down a bit, more on purpose than unintentionally. After all, one never pays the payroll with any intent of a rosy future. Besides, as you will freely admit, the Emporium itself bound our minds to it, and work took over whenever there was the slightest chance for us to get in any way – er – intimate."

At the sound of the word intimate, Hector folded, unfolded and refolded his napkin. Jean, who felt for an instant that maybe she'd said too much, turned her coffee cup around in its saucer. She decided to herself that, in actual fact, there had been nothing wrong with what she had just said – after all, if not now, when exactly would such an opportunity ever present itself.

Hector was looking intently at her, so she, in turn, looked around the restaurant at the various tables and their occupants before remarking, "They're busy tonight, aren't they?"

He was still looking deeply into her eyes, so returning the soft but fixed gaze, she rested her elbows on the table and laid her head lightly on her raised and cupped hands.

"A penny for your thoughts?" she asked.

He smiled, the creases in his face softened by the candlelight. "I think it's now a priority for certain things to take over the top spot in my life from the Gem Emporium. Simply by going to England, losing Thomas and gaining Barbara and Stuart, life has shown me that there are still a myriad of emotions to enjoy rather than to fear or despise. Age is supposed to generate wisdom rather than bitterness, and I cannot help but think that in years to come, with nothing but the Emporium to hold in my hand, I would become a lonely and bitter old man. Fate, through the actions taken by Lee Eng Tek, has given me the shake-up I needed to place into a better perspective the more important things in my life, which, up until now, were demoted to a lesser status than they should ever have been. What I mean, of course, is us. We both, in essence, come from the same background, and generally we both enjoy the same things. As for romance, I tend to think we come from a time when real romance was spelt out with actions and feelings, rather than with words and great declarations." He sipped his coffee and continued playing with his napkin, which had by now taken on the mantle of comfort blanket. She had sat perfectly still, listening to his every word, and, true to the legion of womanhood, had not given a thing away, be it positive or, for that matter, negative.

"Like so many people in the rat-race world of city life today, we spend more time together during daylight hours than we would otherwise do with a partner after working hours. Since, in our case, the days seem to work perfectly for us both, what would you say to sharing the evenings and nights with me too?"

That said, he produced a small red velvet box from his pocket. He laid it on the table next to Jean's coffee cup, before sitting back in his chair and holding his breath.

She picked up the box, opened it discreetly, looked at the contents, and, snapping the box shut, put it back down on the table. "I think" she said casually, "that, when all is said and done, whatever happens, it'll be for the best."

Hector felt more like a confused teenager than he ever had done, and that included the time he had spent actually being a teenager all those wasted years ago.

Meanwhile, Barbara and Stuart, both keen to squeeze as much out of Singapore as it would allow them, had returned to Newton Circus, where they sat at a concrete table and ate heartily.

The sounds of local music coming from a radio on one of the food stalls mingled with the loud conversation being bandied about between the locals. Traffic made a steady flow around them, and the flowers and shrubs around them danced lightly in a puff of breeze, sending the fragrance of jasmine across to where they were sat.

The overbearing fragrance coming from a sizzling wok on one of the stalls quickly stifled the jasmine, but, Barbara had to admit to herself as she sat there, she was pleased that they had come all this way. Looking across at Stuart, who by now had recovered quite well and was busily slurping some soup and noodles from a bowl, she was glad he had come too. It had, without a doubt, opened his eyes up to the wealth of a world ripe for discovery, and nudged him to realise that there were more places to see than the tired and well-trodden run-of-the-mill Spanish resorts.

"We'll have to get a wok when we go home. I'm sure we can create some of the dishes they've got here almost the same way."

Stuart looked at her and stabbed a prawn with his chopsticks. "Well, it would certainly bring a cultural feel to the Bide-a-Wee, wouldn't it?" and they laughed. "Bonnie would be driven crazy by the smells, and would probably be sat permanently to attention in the kitchen waiting for you to drop or drip something in her direction."

Barbara smiled and then sighed. The smile disappeared as quickly as it had arrived. "I'll tell you a secret: I'm tired of that place. If I'm honest, now that we have the means, I'd rather like us to start out again somewhere fresh, not in Boscombe, but maybe in Poole. After all, we've got all our friends in the area, so it wouldn't make sense to move completely away. But, I do feel that our days of doing bed-and-breakfast catering are over. Tommy would want us to enjoy life a bit now anyway. Don't you think?" She sucked on a straw, and smacked her lips at the taste of fresh watermelon juice.

Stuart chewed thoughtfully for a few minutes, while Barbara made noises of ecstasy as she devoured her chicken satay. Finishing his last prawn, he rested his chopsticks and wiped his hands on a refresher towel that Barbara had magically produced from her handbag. "I'll tell you a secret," he said: "I agree with you entirely about the demise of the Bide-a-Wee, and can envisage us in a nice new home near Poole Harbour, only I insist we name it aptly. I was wondering what you thought of the name Sentosa being painted next to the letter box?"

Barbara clapped her hands. "Perfect! And, I'm sure you'll agree it's a step up from the Ponderosa we've been used to."

Laughter again filled the air, and they turned their attention to the seeking-out of something sweet to have after their meal.

The following morning arrived quietly in Hector's apartment. Stuart lay in bed staring at the ceiling. It was early, and he thought to himself what an experience Singapore had been. A breeze wafted into the room, billowing the thin curtain like a spinnaker, and Stuart stirred out of his daydream.

Getting out of bed, he perched on the corner of it and stared at his suitcase, packed and almost ready for travel. Noise from the kitchen announced that someone was up, so he pulled a silk dressing gown around himself, admired the dragon motif on the back of it in a mirror, and ventured out into the dining room in search of coffee and nicotine.

He found Hector sat on the balcony cuddling a mug of green tea and watching the city wake up to a new day.

"A fine day, isn't it? – for a last one, that is," Stuart said as he sat down next to Hector, taking a slurp from his coffee.

Hector didn't react, and seemed to be locked miles away within himself.

"Are you okay?" Stuart gently asked. "After all, tomorrow we'll be gone and you'll have your domain back to yourself."

Hector sipped his green tea and turned his gaze towards Stuart. "That's just it! I don't want it all to myself. I've had enough of a self-imposed exiled existence. Both of you dropping into my life the way you have, through Thomas's intervention, has changed that. Besides, don't be under any misapprehension that I'll be glad to wave you off at Changi tonight – I shan't be."

Stuart pulled his knees up and rested his chin on them. "Well, the thing is that although you'll be here, and we'll be there, it's not the distance that's important, but the fact that now, after this adventure of a trip we've had, we all know that we aren't on our own. From now on we'll be in regular contact with each other, and there'll be more trips for you to the UK, and more visits to this wonderful place for us."

Hector sighed. "Believe me, I'm very mindful of that, and really appreciate the bond that we've formed. It's your father's legacy, and, as such, will never be broken. What you don't know is that last night I proposed to Jean."

Stuart smiled. "And?"

Hector fingered the corner of his newspaper nervously. "That's it, you see. She didn't say. I'm in that state of limbo – waiting. It's not nice, I have to tell you."

Stuart took the newspaper, and, licking his finger, opened it at the crossword page. "Well, sitting here stewing in your juice over it all isn't going to change anything. She'll let you know in her own time. So, meanwhile, put your thinking cap on and let's kill this crossword."

There they sat, huddled together over the table, deep in thought, together with the *Straits Times*, until a rasping hoppity cough from the kitchen made them jump, and it became apparent that Barbara was meeting the day head on.

Jean's home was a neat and well-laid-out apartment. Although smaller than Hector's penthouse, it was placed in a good locality, and over the years had established itself as a cocoon away from the fast pace at which Singapore so readily speeds through life. There were plants everywhere, which, to anyone who knew her well, indicated that they were Jean's family. A large chesterfield sofa was placed in the middle of the lounge, and framed prints of English countryside watercolours adorned the walls. There was no television, but a very good-quality hi-fi system and radio, which regularly played music for the plants' benefit as well as Jean's. The television, a small one, was in the bedroom, and really only in use for CNN broadcasts. From time to time, she could be found curled up with laughter whilst watching some British comedy, but it was rare.

The kitchen was longer than it was wide, and, noting its similarity to a galley on board a yacht, Jean had given it a nautical flavour, with decor picked up along the path of life from islands she had visited. Living on an island, she liked to share this fact with other island-dwellers around the world. There seemed to be a familiar association between island folk. Of course, nobody told her that to compare Singapore with the Isle of Wight or Tasmania was like comparing Verdi's opera with Bulgarian folk-dancing music.

Nevertheless, Jean was content in her little palace. There was a small balcony, just large enough for a table and two chairs. The climate gave vibrant and vivid life to the myriad of plants that grew in profusion; as she sat amid all the foliage with a tea tray on the table, listening to a selection of arias, Jean contemplated her life as a single, and also the prospect of being half of a couple. It had not been an image that had settled easily with her initially, but, having had a near sleepless night, the idea had grown on her. Gremlins from the past were in fact, as she suddenly realised, just that – in the past. It was unfair to tar all men with the same brush, and she knew that under his crusty exterior Hector had a sensitive and caring side to him, though it was realistic to note that it was well hidden. Then there was the issue of nerves. Having been single for so long, she was a very individual and independent lady – the mere idea of having to envisage sharing things and giving way to certain discussions made her flush. However, at the bottom of it all, under the nerves and all the gremlins, she knew in her heart of hearts that she loved him.

She rinsed the teapot as Madam Butterfly declared the loves, sorrows and hopes of 'One Fine Day', and put the china back in its home in the cupboard next to her selection of teas. Opening a drawer, she laid a teaspoon back in its compartment with its brothers and sisters, and stood quite still staring at the cutlery. A dessert spoon was facing the wrong way and made everything look out of place. She turned it round, so that all at once everything became neat. 'That settles it,' she thought to herself, and, after powdering her nose quickly in the mirror by the front door, she picked up her handbag and left home, heading for the Emporium.

Hector was sat at his desk surrounded by faxes, invoices and contracts. In an attempt to calm his mind, he had put a CD on, and was listening to 'Songs of the Auvergne' as he sorted piles of papers into order of priority.

The lift pinged, and he heard movement outside his office. "Is that you, Jean?" he asked, almost swallowing a breath.

Barbara and Stuart staggered into the office, laden down with bags of shopping – evidence of their last-minute panic buying.

"Oh, God, my feet!" puffed Barbara. "I think my bunions know every step of Orchard Road by now."

Stuart collapsed into a chair, glossy bags all around him. "She forgets I'm still in recovery! But, oh no, we had to go round the stores one last time, and then down to Raffles Plaza to finish off. How we're going to get it all home I can't begin to imagine."

"I wouldn't worry about that, Stuart. I've booked a car to meet you at Heathrow in the morning and drive you home, so there'll be someone to help you and plenty of room to stow your bags."

Jean had arrived, and stood in the doorway to Hector's office with a tray of champagne and glasses. "Just about time for a farewell drink, I think, don't you?"

Stuart's weariness evaporated instantly. Jumping to his feet, he ran over to Jean. Taking the tray from her, he pecked her on the cheek. "You're an angel. Thanks for organising that for us. Hector, I hope you know what a wonder you have for an assistant?"

Hector nodded and set about pouring the champagne.

Being offered a glass by Hector, Jean curled her fingers around the stem, and raised her glass. "A toast, I think – to us, to the future, and, of course, to Thomas."

Everyone raised their glasses and said, "Cheers," except Hector, who, mid-sip and mid-toast, had noticed that Jean was wearing the engagement ring he had given her the previous evening.

The sapphire winked at him, and he leaned over to Jean, kissing her softly on the cheek. "To us, as well, and our future," he murmured.

Stuart, having spotted the ring when he had relieved Jean of the tray, couldn't contain himself a moment longer. "About bloody time! A second toast, then – to you two, and many more cruises to Sentosa together."

They laughed, and Barbara fizzed enthusiastically – almost as much as the champagne in her glass, which was going down a treat after all that shopping.

With everything packed, and an extra suitcase purchased on the way home to Hector's to accommodate all the extra shopping, they piled into a car and were driven through the busy evening traffic to Changi Airport.

Approaching it along a straight highway, down the centre of which grew beautiful plants and flowers, Barbara realised that she was now going home, and began to cry quietly.

Stuart squeezed an arm round her. "All good things come to an end. Besides, imagine how pleased Bonnie will be to see us."

She patted her face with a small handkerchief, and, asking Jean for the loan of her compact, powdered her nose gently to affect some repair work to her make-up. "I know you're right, of course – it's just that I can't bear farewells."

Taking her compact back, Jean corrected her. "But it's not farewell, merely au revoir."

The business-class check-in counter handled them swiftly and courteously, just as Stuart would have expected, and he couldn't help but smile to himself at seeing the name Raffles written above the counter.

Bags sent and boarding passes in hand, they all adjourned to a bar, where Barbara checked and rechecked several times that she had the passports and tickets safely tucked away in her handbag.

A pause in conversation noted that it would be a while before the four of them would be together again, and they just sat in silence looking and smiling at one another. Anyone passing by would have wondered as to the combined sanity of the foursome, but, of course, it does little justice to the image if you don't know the whole history behind people.

It was getting late in the evening. Flights were departing for far-off destinations, with calls going out for stragglers and strays to hurry to their gates for immediate departure. The digital-display screen blinked 'boarding' next to the flight number and destination 'London'.

So, getting to his feet, Stuart looked at Barbara and said, "Come on, then, we should leave these lovebirds and head for the gate. I'm not having a strained voice calling out my name, hinting that it's solely me that's causing delays for the airline."

Barbara hugged Hector, and then Jean, before Stuart swept both Hector and Jean together into one big hug. "You're right, Jean, it is only au revoir; so, until the next meeting of the glee club, look after each other."

With that, he linked arms with Barbara, and they made their way through the security checkpoint, where she held up the queue whilst fishing in her handbag for the passports. Then, with arms waving from both directions, they parted, and Hector and Jean took their car back into the city.

Barbara looked out of the window as the jumbo took off, and watched as all the twinkling lights of the city floated away from her. "Goodbye," she whispered as a tear escaped down her cheek. Turning to Stuart, who was busy selecting his choice of meal from the menu, and deciding which wine to accompany it, she nestled into his shoulder and asked, "So, what's for dinner, then?"

Chapter Nine

There's No Place Like Home

To say that Bonnie was delighted to see Barbara and Stuart would have been somewhat of an understatement. The little pug jumped, barked, and hopped from one paw to the other.

She was so excited that the vicar's wife wondered if the dog might self-combust at any moment. With that said, she left the doorstep of the Bide-a-Wee under the heavily veiled excuse of being "Awfully late for a hair appointment."

Barbara had invited her to wait a while, so that she might find, buried somewhere in the luggage, a gift which she had bought by way of a thank you for looking after Bonnie.

The vicar's wife, however, was in a flurry of twitches and fidgets, and said there was no need, and that they would be sure to see one another at the next jumble sale. Waddling away from the front door, she declared to herself adamantly that the idea of her and the vicar ever getting a dog would be, henceforth, for ever banished from their minds. Besides, a cat would be easier to look after. She liked cats.

Barbara was staring at her suitcase, knowing how heavy it was, and what a long job there was ahead of her to unpack, wash clothes and reorganise life back again on the home front. She sat on the Elvis sofa cuddling an Elvis cushion, and looked around her.

Stuart came into the lounge with a tray of tea, just in time to hear her expel a deep sigh. "That's not a good sign, dear one," he said as he passed her a mug of hot English tea. "Get that inside you. You'll feel much better. It's proper real tea, just the way we like it – none of your foreign stuff with petals in it. It almost looked more like potpourri than tea, didn't it? Besides, we're home now. It's been quite a trip. Just think how everyone will enjoy hearing about it. Can you imagine what Dale will say when we tell him about the adventures of Bonnie Chalmers?"

Barbara would have quite liked to be able to sit down and tell her beloved Tommy about their adventure-filled trip to Singapore with

Hector and Jean. But she couldn't, so instead she blew on her tea and took a sip. Stuart was obviously excited to be home. She, however, was not quite ready to return.

As Stuart fussed Bonnie, who was running circles around his legs and backing up in an effort to tempt the throwing of a squeaky toy, Barbara couldn't help herself but to sit there, her mind stuck on the image of Tommy. It seemed that almost without any effort at all a steady stream of stinging tears trickled their way down her cheek. Feeling unable to control the flow, she ran from the Elvis lounge and fled to her bedroom, where she lay on her bed crying into the pillow for the rest of the afternoon.

Stuart didn't quite know what to do with himself. It was, he eventually concluded, the time for grieving, which, with everything that had happened before, had been delayed by the trip to Singapore.

Bonnie stood in the hall, hopefully staring at her tartan leash, which hung from the banister. Sensing that for Barbara it was a time to be left on her own, Stuart conceded to Bonnie that it was as good a time as any to go for a long walk along the cliff top and down to the shore.

Together they left, with Bonnie tugging and choking the way ahead to an exotic selection of smells that, apparently, drives dogs insane.

Barbara sat up. She had heard the front door close, and knew that she had the place to herself for a while. That felt like a first. The only thing missing was her Tommy. It dawned on her that, having had Hector around her for several weeks, there had still been that attachment to Tommy. Now, with Hector so far away, the house screamed in silence at her, a bit like that messy but much talked-about piece of modern art which she had seen a picture of in the in-flight magazine on the way home. Everywhere she looked was daubed with memories of Tommy.

The phone rang. She contemplated ignoring it, but, after a few rings, she hauled herself off the bed with a lot of effort and stomped downstairs, picking up the phone and lighting a cigarette at the same time.

There was a brief crackle on the line, and then Jean's voice came crisply out of the void. "Hello, Barbara, we're just checking you two got home safely, and Hector wants to have a word. I'll be in touch later, but stay on the line, I'm connecting you to him now."

Barbara blew her nose during the pause. She was still wiping her top lip when Hector boomed down the telephone. "Did you get back okay? I just want you to know how quiet it is without you. I'm still getting used to having to try to do the crossword by myself again. Listen, I need you to get in touch with a Neil Newman, who it turned out was Thomas's solicitor."

"Oh, yes, I remember him. Lots of spit flying everywhere when he speaks, and a distinct taint of nicotine about him," Barbara replied as she stabbed the cigarette out in an ashtray next to the phone. "I think I can remember where his office is, so I'll call him and go to see him, if that's what you want, dear."

Hector doodled on his desk pad and turned his mind to other things. "It's okay, Jean has his address and telephone numbers, they were on the envelope he gave me at the funeral. I'll get her to make an appointment for you, say, the day after tomorrow? Let me know what transpires with Mr Newman. If there's any help needed, I'll do whatever is required. Hopefully, Thomas hasn't left any more surprises for us. Anyway, Jean will be in touch with you about a date for our wedding. We both want you to come over, although it'll be no great flamboyant event – just a small affair, but we hope it'll be tasteful. After all, it's supposed to be a special day for people, isn't it? no matter what age they are."

Barbara smiled to herself at his awkwardness. He was still grappling with emotions that had been hidden away for so long. "Well, I'll talk to Stuart and Jean, and we'll make plans. Give my love to Singapore, and we'll keep in touch. I'll let you know if anything needs attention after seeing Neil Newman."

They said their goodbyes, and Barbara returned to the comfort, security and solitude of her bedroom.

All of a sudden, Stuart realised that it was still mid-winter on the south coast of England. Once Bonnie had dragged him to the cliff top, where they now stood looking at the sea together, why it was that the heat and humidity of Singapore seemed so far off was difficult to pinpoint. Everything had sped along at a huge rate of knots, and he took a while to think about the fact that Barbara had only now been slapped in the face by the harsh reality of her grief. Bonnie bit the top off a weed that had been growing next to the bench where they were sitting, and sniffed into the wind that blew off the sea. Stuart looked down at her and smiled. "So did you miss us?"

The pug momentarily pricked up her ears, looked at him and blinked. Neither felt compelled to make a move, so, for a while, they continued to sit there looking at the sea and thinking things over. Stuart would have questioned the ethics of genetic linkage had he known that his uncle had done the same thing a few weeks before.

Having followed up Jean's initial appointment, Barbara took the bus into town a few days later. She found herself stood in a corridor outside a small office, on the door of which was painted the name N. Newman, Solicitor.

She knocked and went into a small reception area where an elderly secretary was sat in front of an ancient typewriter. The secretary, whose wild hair held Barbara's gaze for several minutes, answered to the name of Lavinia. She proceeded to eye Barbara suspiciously over the top of her half-moon glasses.

Lavinia had clung onto the more traditional aspect of office work for the better part of her working life, and no amount of training courses offered by Mr Newman had tempted her towards a more modern method of working. Jean would have been horrified at the antiquity of it all, thought Barbara. A door opened and Neil Newman literally spat her name out with a nicotine-edged smile as he ushered her into his office, clearing paperwork from the chair in front of his desk and indicating that she should take a seat.

"So, I believe Mr Barnes returned to Singapore, and that you and your son accompanied him in order to have a bit of a break."

"That's right," said Barbara, who for a heartbeat felt as if she were sat in a witness box in court. "It was lovely. If you haven't been, you really ought to go. It's a marvellous place – and very friendly locals."

Neil winced slightly and rested his elbow on the arm of his chair. "I couldn't go that far. Somewhere hot by the Med is far enough for me."

Barbara thought back for a moment. It wasn't so long ago that she would probably have said something along the same lines herself. She resisted the temptation to share the thought with Neil, composing herself more for the purpose of her visit. If he wanted holiday advice and tips, let him go and chat up the young girl at the travel agency round the corner.

"Was there anything else of Tommy's that needed clearing up? Hector said that if there was, then he would be happy to – um – help."

Neil took out a handkerchief and rummaged around his nose whilst thinking of how he was going to say what he had to say. "Well, the expenses for the funeral were taken care of already by Mr Barnes – Thomas, that is. He left funds for the costs. Otherwise, there's a bank account with not much in it," and, lifting a piece of paper, he traced the figure with his finger. "Four hundred and thirty-three pounds and seventeen pence; in fact. That's about it really. Our fees come to two hundred and forty-five pounds; so, you see, I'm afraid it leaves you somewhat up the proverbial creek without a paddle for any future security."

Barbara uncrossed her legs as pins and needles were beginning to take hold. "I wouldn't quite say . . . " She bit her tongue, thinking it best to keep quiet about money. It might be difficult to explain. Nobody would believe the story if she told them. Instead, she sighed dramatically and returned Neil's somewhat strained gaze. 'Poor thing, he must be gasping for a ciggie,' she thought. "I'm sure we'll get through. After all, at a time like this it's not money you miss, it's the – um – dearly departed we still lay a place for at the dinner table, isn't it?"

Neil rose to his feet and extended his hand. "I appreciate it must be a difficult time, but good luck for the future. If you need my services, you know where I am."

'Too right I do –' thought Barbara to herself, 'propping up the bar in the Red Lion.' She smiled and said, "Thank you, Neil. You're very kind."

She sailed out of the office and ran a short distance to catch a bus into the town centre. There she opened an account at the main department store, and had lunch in their brasserie on the fourth floor.

On her way home she stopped outside an estate agency, and browsed for a full ten minutes, before going inside to get some details.

As the last notes of *La Bohème* faded away, Jean lifted her feet off the sofa and drank the last gulp of malt whisky from her crystal tumbler. Some large leaves on the balcony bounced up and down in a warm evening breeze, nodding their approval of the evening's choice of musical entertainment. She removed the CD and inserted a fresh one, forwarding it to the final couple of tracks. She pressed play before heading for the bathroom, where she washed, cleansed and brushed, all in time to *The Mikado*.

Lying in bed, she mused about how much a creature of habit she was, and she wondered if having Hector share her life would create friction. They were both long-term singles and, as such, would there be problems in the realignment of their karmas?

Hector sat in the dark. He liked sitting in the dark. You could see all the lights of the city much better, and pick out little bits of people's lives to watch from afar. Nevertheless, it would be a good habit to get out of when faced with the alternative of a soft, full-figured lady waiting to cuddle up with in the bedroom. Besides, he had spent quite a long time sat in the dark, thanks to the courtesy of Lee Eng Tek, and that had rather taken the shine off one of his hitherto favourite pastimes.

Thankfully, the Singapore Police had noted all the details he could muster in his statement, and, despite it taking slightly longer than he would have liked, they had eventually caught Alex; and, after several lengthy interviews, they had been able to trace Miss Lim to a hotel in the far north of Thailand. As for Lee himself, Hector decided that he had probably melted away into one of the less sociable corners of Asia. Having abandoned Miss Lim to take the full force of the charges on her own shoulders, he would no doubt surface one day. Hector would be sure to be ready for him then.

Meanwhile, there were plans to be finalised for the wedding, so, with a contented grin and sigh, he whistled his way through his own ablutions before jumping into bed and searching out the cooler corners of the mattress with his feet. This was all very different to Vicky's bed, where he would have done almost anything for a spot of Singaporean heat. "Oh, Christ!" he said out loud, "I'll have to invite them to the wedding."

The front porch of the Bide-a-Wee was a complete mess. Both Stuart and Bonnie thought so. As they stood there while Stuart fumbled in his pocket for the key, they looked around at the assorted clutter, which over the years had found a home in the porch. Bonnie sniffed, stretching her neck into the corners, looking almost like a forest pig snuffling for truffles.

"When are we going to clear the porch out? There's one big holy pile of crap there, and hardly any of it belongs to us," Stuart said. He picked up a pair of mud-clogged shoes that had at one time been described as sensible, and a shopping bag stuffed full with scrunched-up shopping bags, both of which he carried through the kitchen and out to the dustbin on the rear patio.

It was on his return to the kitchen that he sniffed, as Bonnie did simultaneously, and, looking at each other, they both trotted over to Barbara, who was making heavy work of chopping, seasoning and stir-frying their meal in a shiny new wok.

"I got it on the way home. Now we can bring a bit of Singapore to our own home for a touch of cooking experimentation. It can't be that difficult. They do it all the time on TV, and we saw it often enough over there, didn't we?" With that, she wiped her brow on her sleeve, and with a final flourish of stir, sprinkle and stir again, she emptied the contents of the wok onto two plates, and proudly carried them to the dining room.

They sat eating in silence. Bonnie wasn't a huge fan of oriental food. The scent of ginger and lemon grass infusing together made her eyes smart, so she retreated to her knitted blanket in the corner of the Elvis lounge.

"It's very nice," Stuart lied.

Barbara took a sip of her rosé wine and, swallowing hard, admitted with a smile of accepted defeat, "Come off it, it's horrid. Never mind the mixture of ingredients, which I'll have to read up on a bit more, it's just not the same as having this type of food in the authentic surroundings, is it?"

They laughed and toasted each other to the first use of the wok.

Stuart made coffee, and, sitting down in the Elvis lounge, noticed the large envelope on the table. Barbara followed his gaze, so she handed him the selection of property portfolios that she had collected from the estate agency in town.

"Have a look at these. I'm sure there's a Sentosa somewhere among them, just waiting for us to take up residence."

She lit a cigarette and studied his face. It was one of the things that, as his mother, she could always get a lot of feedback from. She knew her son well enough to tell by the mildest frown, sparkle or twitch whether he rated something or not. It was always a good gauge to go by, since he had such a good eye and a clarity of thought and resonance, which she recognised as lacking in herself.

As she watched, he read and digested the dozen or so sheets of paper and sorted them into three piles. Once finished, he sat back in the armchair, folding his arms, and looked at Barbara. "Eight are non-starters. Either they're too old, and as such would need too much spending on them to renovate, or they're too far from the shops. One of them would be fine if it wasn't for the location – next door to a primary school on one side and a takeaway on the other. One word for you, my dear: 'rats' on both\sides. It's not for us. So, that leaves three to go and have a look at."

He passed her the three portfolios, and she sat reading through them while he watched a television programme about a couple from Leeds who were in search of their ideal home on the north coast of Cornwall.

Almost as an afterthought, it was only when they both climbed the stairs to bed that night that Stuart suddenly said, "Oh! How did you get on with Neil Newman? Where there any problems?"

Barbara smiled slightly. "No, dear, everything was fine. But I rather thought he was fishing for a widow's hidden fortune. He was far too smarmy for my liking. Still, it's over and done with, so there'll be no further need for Mr Newman. Goodnight, darling."

They hugged and kissed each other, and, with a flick of a switch on the landing, the house fell into darkness. The silence was punctuated by the delicate snores of a pug in twitching mid-dream cycle on the end of Stuart's bed.

A few days later they had viewed two out of the three homes on offer. The estate agent was driven by the aim to please, and, in this case, she was beginning to take the whole thing personally. There would be a sale agreed, otherwise her name wasn't Charlotte. She always got her quarry, and had acquired somewhat of a heady reputation in the district as one not to mess with. As such, it was only occasionally that she crossed swords with a new recruit from a competitor. She always triumphed, leaving the young jock to sit in a dazed and confused state at his desk for several days, wondering how the hell she had got one over on him.

She was tall, striking and shrewd, and Stuart adored her from the moment he clapped eyes on her. Barbara thought that Charlotte had "a very nice tone of voice, and a lovely way of explaining things in a way that I can understand".

They had seen the inside of the house, and were stood on a long patio which ran off from sliding doors outside the lounge. A sloping terraced lawn ran down to some shrubs and borders, drawing the eye to a small fishpond, complemented by a trickling water feature. It was plain to see that the current owners loved their garden, and had spent a lot of time and money on it.

What eventually clinched the sale, as indeed Charlotte knew it would do, was the sight of Poole Harbour that came into view as they walked along the patio. Despite it being a grey February afternoon, the harbour, one of the largest natural harbours in the world, and, for many people, on a par with Sydney, looked beautiful. Barbara and Stuart twittered between themselves like two excited sparrows, getting more enthused by the minute. Charlotte just stood back and leaned against the wall. Her job was done.

Hector rather wished that his job was done too. How was it, that to plan a small wedding (with the emphasis on small) had transpired to be such a mission. Jean had been sweet enough to say that she would be happy with whatever he arranged. If that wasn't women's talk for 'get on with it, but if it isn't to my liking, there'll be trouble', he didn't know what was.

The only stipulation from her was that there should be peach-coloured roses, and no orchids. "After all," she had purred one evening, "we are British, not Singaporean."

This, he had reckoned, would be the easiest of his tasks. Wrong! There were roses on offer of every colour – some fresh yellow ones, some pure white ones, and some rich dark-red ones. Peach-coloured ones, however, were in scant supply, and would have to be flown in the day before the wedding itself, which immediately put Hector on edge. What if they didn't arrive? One simple request from her, and it was already turning into the floral equivalent of a request for a papal blessing and a knighthood from Her Majesty.

St Andrew's Cathedral had been booked for the service at two in the afternoon, music had been selected, and a reception had been negotiated with the Elizabeth Hotel, which would take place in their Langtry Lobby Lounge after the service.

All his plans began to take shape as the day approached, and Hector found himself rushing around C. K. Tang's in pursuit of the final touches to his arrangements. He had visited his tailor, chosen material for a suit, been measured, and gone to great lengths to assure the tailor that he really was getting married, even at his age.

Jean had taken a day off work to go in search of her own wedding attire. Happy with her choices, she treated herself to the new experience of a spa session at the Pan Pacific Hotel.

After discussing the guest list with Hector one morning, they had decided on keeping the numbers down – just close friends and family, a total of thirty-two guests. They would have invited more, but, after Hector had related the tale of the sceptic tailor, they were both somewhat dubious of people's reactions to the fact that two high-profile members of Singapore's longest serving singles community were now tying the knot. It had been concluded that there would be a function held at the Gem Emporium when they returned from their honeymoon. That way, all the business associates of Hector's, coupled with Jean's network of friends and acquaintances from the diplomatic corps, could mingle together, and deal en masse with the sight of the happy and freshly married couple's return.

The only thing to get co-ordinated was the arrival at Changi of people who were flying in for the wedding. Stuart, Barbara, Bob and Vicky were all coming on the same flight from London. Jean's cousin was coming from New Zealand, and the godchildren and a couple of friends were due to land from Melbourne an hour later. Cars were booked to collect them all and install them in the hotel. There would be drinks and nibbles the night before the wedding.

Hector felt himself finally relax as he lay in bed the night before all the international arrivals, taking comfort in the fact that, when it came to wedding rings, his Emporium could produce something that would tingle Jean's senses all the way to Cape Town, where they would be spending their honeymoon.

Chapter Ten

Cocktails with a Twist

All the flights landed without any problems or delays. The wedding guests were collected from the arrivals hall and driven to the Elizabeth Hotel. They checked in, and all went straight to their rooms to freshen up after their long flights.

Stuart and Barbara led the way wherever they got the chance, since they were now seasoned travellers and had previous experience of Singapore. This proved invaluable, if for no other reason than it had helped to deter Vicky from asking whoever would listen to her who it was that Barbara thought she was to play Lady Muck. After all, just because they had flown economy, whilst Stuart and Barbara had enjoyed another Raffles experience, why should they think they took prime spot with everything? Inevitably though, it had been Vicky who, with Bob struggling behind her with their luggage, had stayed close to Barbara from the moment they had met on the air bridge after getting off the aircraft.

A few hours later Hector and Jean arrived at the hotel. They had reserved a table for dinner, so that everyone should get to know one another before the wedding itself.

Hearing raucous laughter coming from a bar, Jean looked at Hector and said, "It looks like my bunch of Antipodeans are having a pre-dinner drink. I'll go in and join them. You go up and check on Stuart and Barbara. See how they're getting on with Bob and Vicky." She giggled, knowing that she ought not to have done, but she couldn't help herself. After what he had told her about Vicky, she was curious to see the chemistry evolve.

Hector pecked her on the cheek. "Get a whisky ready for me. I'll be back down in a few minutes."

Knocking on the room door, he heard a hair dryer whine down to a stop. The door was flung open and Stuart stood in the entrance of the room, draped in towels, complete with a towel twisted into a pinnacle around his head. He had twisted it so tight that it pulled the skin around his eyes up and gave him a faintly oriental look.

"How you doin'?" he asked. He threw his arms around Hector, giving him a big hug, which, much to his surprise, Hector found totally enjoyable.

Barbara was puffing and swearing, trying to pull a new pair of shoes on, and, from what he could see, Hector deduced that trouble was afoot. He chuckled at his own pun, drawing a look of venom from her.

"It's not my fault that my ankles have swollen, even after that lovely flight. How are you, dear? Give me a kiss, but be careful not to smudge my make-up."

Hector traced around the bottom of the bedspread with his shoe, and asked, "So, have you got to know Bob and Vicky yet?"

Barbara sat up, preferring to struggle with the shoe by wriggling her ankle. As she gave some effort to push her foot into the shoe, she blew out with a puff of energy: "Vicky?" She lit a cigarette before continuing. "Personally, it's just because she's your oldest friend's wife that I'm keeping mum and being nice. Stuart has started calling her Sicky."

Stuart untwisted the towel and looked up. "What? Well, she is a real pain, I reckon. How Bob has put up with it for so long leaves me bloody speechless and nearly suicidal at the spectacle."

Hector looked at him. "Of course, love takes many forms, doesn't it?"

Stuart blushed and went off to decide which shirt to wear, and which one of his duty-free fragrances to spray himself with.

"At the end of the day, they're not exactly well-travelled folks, and, although I know only too well how – um – difficult she can be at times, it's Bob who has always been such a loyal and dependable friend. So, for the sake of that, please try and get along with her." Hector played with a cufflink, hoping that what he had said would hit the mark.

During this plea, Barbara sprayed hairspray at length, and Stuart stood in front of the bathroom mirror, also spraying at length. They linked arms and stood before Hector. "Don't fret. We'll be exactly how you want us to be."

Hector frowned. "Oh, I don't mean to sound that harsh. Enjoy yourselves. Just cut Vicky a bit of slack, that's all."

"Come along," smiled Barbara, "we read you loud and clear. Now let's go and get a drink. I'm dying for one of those Singapore slings."

They found Jean surrounded by a selection of Australians and New Zealanders, creased up with laughter at yet another joke from her godchild's partner.

Bob and Vicky were sat at a small table by the window, looking at the water feature in the manicured garden area outside. To Stuart's credit, it wasn't long before he had cajoled Vicky over to the Australians, and the New Zealanders found that they bonded remarkably quickly with Bob. His quiet manner, and the knack of imparting a teasing and naughty story in a way that, if viewed from afar, you would think he was giving some compassionate solace, won him friends quickly. Even the Australians, who, as is their nature, enjoy teasing the British as a national sport, realised that here was someone that they wanted to have among their number, rather than as an object for ridicule.

Dinner went well. People chatted, and, with Hector and Jean bobbing up and down to mingle throughout the meal, a friendly and relaxed atmosphere ensured that good food and good company were the order of the day, just as Hector had wished it.

The morning broke calmly for most, yet with the thump of a hangover for a few – Vicky among them.

Jean had asked her and the cousin from New Zealand, Noreen, to go with her to the hairdressers for styling and manicure, and then to get dressed together at her apartment before the car would arrive to take them to the cathedral.

Hector had gathered Bob, Stuart and a couple of Australians together, and they were having brunch on his balcony before getting ready to go to the cathedral too.

The phone rang, and Stuart answered it as he finished pouring the final glass of Dom Perignon into his flute glass.

Hector was stood quite still in his bedroom while Bob fiddled with a cravat that wouldn't behave itself around Hector's neck.

"That was the florist. They've got the peach-coloured roses in, and have decorated in the cathedral for you, just as you requested. The bouquet is being delivered to Jean now." Stuart sipped his champagne, and, having delivered the message, left the room in search of some more.

Hector beamed. "She'll be delighted. It was the only thing she asked for, and, believe you me, it took some ordering and searching, but now that it's done, nothing can go wrong."

Bob smiled, looked down his nose at the cravat, and passed Hector fit for presentation to his bride in the cathedral.

Of course, it's the worst thing to say on a wedding day: 'nothing can go wrong'.

Across the city, the florist replaced the phone on its hook, and she took her envelope of money before handing over the keys to her van and leaving for the day.

Nobody, least of all Miss Lim herself, would have believed it possible for such a vast sum of money to be paid for bail. So it was that, having resigned herself to a lengthy jail term, whilst curled up in her cell a prison officer had rattled her cell door, unlocked it and led her out into the hands of a lawyer. Lee Eng Tek's legal affairs were always known to be in good hands, and, as such, with Lee's financial backing, the bail had been posted, allowing Miss Lim to feel the sun on her shoulders once more.

As they drove into the city, the lawyer passed her a mobile phone, and she listened intently to the instructions that were given. This time, she would not fail in her mission.

The florist had been easy to track down. Such a large consignment of roses being flown into Changi's cargo terminal had been easy to follow, and one of Lee's hidden spies had checked the shipment papers, phoning the details of the florist through to Lee before he had called to speak with Miss Lim.

The car had dropped her off, and, after a little persuasion, the florist had been bought off for the day. She inspected the small bouquet, and, opening the small clutch bag that had been handed to her by Lee's lawyer. She produced a small vial, and, breaking the seal, proceeded to pour drops of the deadly poison into the roses, so that the droplets ran deep into the leaves and completely infiltrated the arrangement.

Pleased with her handiwork, Miss Lim put on the cotton jacket that staff from the florist wore as a kind of uniform, complete with a bright-pink orchid on the lapel. She carried the bouquet outside to the delivery van. The traffic, though fairly busy, was at least mobile, so it didn't take her long to reach Jean's apartment building.

The ladies had been offered tea, then sherry by Jean. With no takers, she had adjourned to her bedroom to change, and Vicky had taken it upon herself to sniff out something from the drinks cabinet underneath the hi-fi that would mix with one of the selection of fruit juices chilling in the fridge.

The doorbell rang, making her jump and bang her head inside the cabinet. A tinkling of glassware and bottles made her hold her breath for a second. It would be a nightmare if something got broken and she was discovered on her hands and knees looking for alcohol. What would they think?

Noreen came from Jean's bedroom and opened the door to the apartment. A muffled but brief exchange could be heard. Then the door closed and Noreen carried the bouquet through to the bedroom, where Jean's face lit up at the sight of the peach-coloured roses.

"He remembered! How lovely they are too!"

Noreen smiled. "They are, and the florist said the perfume is quite unique."

"Is that so?" Jean said. She was about to lift the bouquet to her nose when a loud crash came from her lounge, followed by a shriek and a string of swear words never before heard in Jean Cutting's home. The bouquet was dropped onto the bed, and both Jean and Noreen rushed from the bedroom, eager to see what the commotion was.

What greeted them was the rear end of Vicky trying to reverse out of the drinks cabinet. The strong smell of gin surrounded her and gave the game away.

"Oh, bugger!" Vicky wailed. "My dress is ruined, and I was only trying to get something to make cocktails for us to enjoy before we leave." She blubbed, and a ruddy blush spread over her face, leaving her to look like a leaking beetroot.

Jean took her by the arm into the bathroom, where, with a bit of nifty work with a flannel and some tepid water, the gin was sponged out of Vicky's dress, and some face-cleansing spray was administered.

Ten minutes later they emerged giggling. They found Noreen stood in the kitchen taking sips from three different coloured drinks, trying to deduce which was the nicest. On being discovered, she roared with laughter, and together they toasted the final hour of Ms Cutting, and wished all good things for the future of the soon-to-be Mrs Barnes.

Amidst some pleasant small talk, with backing music supplied by a CD of Acker Bilk playing 'Stranger on the Shore', they were about to test Noreen's number three cocktail when the telephone rang.

Jean answered it, and almost instantly began flapping like a shirt on the washing line in a strong wind. "The car's here! We have to go. I can't be late. I hope the traffic's not too bad. What if the driver gets lost?"

Vicky picked up Jean's handbag and passed it to her. "Don't worry, love, he'll wait for you, even if you are a bit late."

"Don't forget," declared Noreen in the manner of addressing a whole room full of ladies, rather than just the two that were stood in front of her. "It's a bride's perogati – prerogat – porrotig – oh, hell, she's allowed to be late – it's tradition!"

With that, and a lot of jocular chat, they left the apartment, but not before Vicky had responded to a cry from Jean and rushed back to the bedroom to retrieve the bouquet from the bed.

138

They were on their way, and, as she slammed the door behind her, Vicky was singing, "I'm getting married in the morning" while she sauntered to the elevator, swinging the bouquet by its ribbon.

The men had also had their fair share of Dutch courage. Sat together around the table on Hector's balcony like a jury, they were beginning to sweat under all their suits, and one of the Australians was just beginning to realise that Stuart was not all that he seemed. He had been quiet for the early part of the morning, but, fuelled by two bottles of Dom Perignon, followed by some ice-cold Finnish vodka from Hector's freezer box, he had started sprouting songs by Shirley Bassey and Liza Minnelli. That was all well and good, but to ask the blokes to join in with a chorus from his *Sound of Music* medley was pushing it a bit too far.

Having initially gone for a sulk and a lie-down, Stuart could be heard snoring from a bedroom as Bob looked at his watch and then at Hector. "We'd best all be ready to go. The car's due here any minute now."

Hector left the table, where conversation had turned towards cricket, and went off to rouse Stuart.

The mere fact that as a group they managed to get Stuart sobered up and feeling ready to attend a wedding in just under fifteen minutes was a credit to the assembled past experiences shared between Bob, the Australians and Hector. Having held a sort of testosterone-generated coven, during which all sorts of remedies were mixed and poured down Stuart's throat, they filed down to the waiting car, and soon were on their way to St Andrew's Cathedral.

The window was left down in the back of the car for Stuart's sake, just in case. The breeze, though warm and balmy, helped, and during the journey he gradually came round to his usual chirpy self.

By the time they pulled up outside the cathedral, all was well with the troupe. They walked together as a team in through the main doors, and up the aisle to where the vicar was waiting for them. All that remained to happen now was for the bride herself to turn up.

Jean's car was waiting in a queue of traffic at a major intersection, not too far away. Nonetheless, she kept looking at her watch nervously, and trying her best to smile back at Vicky's glowing and beaming face.

Noreen fished around in her handbag and produced a small brooch, which she pinned to Jean's dress. "They say it's the done thing, you know – something old, something new, something borrowed and something blue. Well, the brooch is Victorian – old; you bought the dress ensemble especially for the wedding – new; I'll have the brooch back later, so it's borrowed; and the stone, as you'll no doubt recognise, is lapis lazuli – so that's the blue bit taken care of." She kissed Jean on the cheek, and Jean smiled.

"That's so clever of you, dear, and very thoughtful."

She fingered the brooch for the remainder of the journey, and, once the car had arrived at the cathedral, Noreen ran inside to alert the gathered crowd and Hector that Jean was where she ought to be, and on time – well, almost!

A light ripple of laughter ran through the small congregation, and the vicar leant over to Hector, just running through the order of service one final time.

Jean walked up the aisle, flanked by Noreen and Vicky, who, at the very last second, remembered that it was Jean who should be holding the bouquet. They passed it to her as she took her place next to Hector for the service.

At the back of the cathedral, Miss Lim hid herself in the shadows. How could it be so, that an English woman like Miss Cutting hadn't taken a moment to smell her wedding bouquet yet?

Gripped by impatience, the often referred-to, and now deservedly nicknamed, 'poisonous Miss Lim' chewed her thumbnail as she willed Jean to take a sniff of her much desired peach roses. It would only need one decent sniff of the flowers, and that would be it.

The florist van was outside ready for a quick getaway, and Lee Eng Tek's lawyers were waiting for her nearby. They were prepared to whisk her across the border to Malaysia, from where a private plane would take her to a retreat far enough removed from the throngs of Singapore, where she would lie low for a few months, until such time as she could resurface and make her play for the Gem Emporium.

Minutes passed by, and the service was in full flow. With still no result for Miss Lim, she could feel a throb of anger brewing from her temples. Finally, her patience ran out. So, with a strangled scream, she ran full speed up the aisle towards Jean and Hector. If events weren't going to run their natural course, she would have to intervene.

Heads turned in open-mouthed shock as the vision of Miss Lim in a bile-induced frenzy surged forward in an attempt to land herself on Jean.

Vicky, who had just finished wiping her eyes and blowing her nose, and who was in the middle of saying to Bob how she always cried at weddings but not at funerals, absent-mindedly placed her handbag by her feet. Since she was sat on the aisle seat of the pew, this instantly put a flaw in Miss Lim's plan. She tripped over the handbag, twisted her ankle, and landed face down at the feet of a stunned vicar. With a contorted face full of hatred, she snarled, flicked her hair, and stared up at a bemused Jean and Hector. "Smell your precious bouquet! The perfume may be sweet, but it'll be the last breath you'll take." Knowing that she had failed again, Miss Lim thumped the carpet and let out a shrill scream of frustrated venom

Jean dropped the bouquet as if it were poisonous which, of course, it was.

As some of the invited guests were diplomats, there were a couple of bodyguards present, so it was thanks to their combined forces and strength that the toxic Miss Lim, screaming for all she was worth, was dragged backwards down the aisle and outside the cathedral to where the police had now arrived to take charge of her.

They checked thoroughly the rest of the flower arrangements in the cathedral before allowing the service to continue. The bouquet was carried carefully away as evidence.

One of Jean's friends, the cultural attache at the Canadian Embassy, untied one of the small arrangements that decorated the end of each pew, and passed it to her.

The closing of the doors echoed throughout the cathedral, and the vicar, taking a deep breath, said in a totally apt and very British manner, "Now then, where were we?"

The remainder of the service passed off without a hitch, and the happy couple, with Hector protectively putting an arm round the shoulders of his bride, passed out of the cathedral and into the late afternoon sunshine.

Applause and a couple of cheers greeted them, and photos were taken. The vicar had asked that confetti be kept to a minimum, as, at his advanced stage in life, the idea of bending over to clear away confetti and rice didn't exactly fill him with Christian goodwill. It also made his knees and one of his hips ache.

People laughed, and together the wedding party made its way back to the Elizabeth Hotel, where food had been prepared and one of Singapore's well-known entertainers was on standby to host a cabaret for the reception.

As is so often the case, the happy couple barely had time to eat anything, or to spend a few minutes with each other. Such as these events are, everyone wants to have time to talk and congratulate, so it was the small hours of the morning before an exhausted Jean and Hector collapsed into bed together. They immediately felt that the right thing had been done, since, cuddled together in bed, there were no words that needed to be spoken. The soft breath and sounds of sleep gave rise to the notion that, for both of them at least, they had been far too long exiled in a wilderness of singledom.

The next morning, guests who had until the wedding been unknown to one another joined up to share breakfast together.

Stuart and Barbara sat at a large round table with some Australians, and a secretary from the South African Embassy arrived for what she described as 'brunch on the run'. Bob and Vicky were surrounded by New Zealanders, Singaporeans and a couple from Hong Kong.

The hum of chatter was at its peak when Hector and Jean arrived, and, amid more rapturous applause, they helped themselves to pastries and fruit juice.

Due to the fact that flights back home to Melbourne, Auckland and, of course, London had all been scheduled for the evening, Jean's last job before the wedding day had been to arrange a sightseeing bus tour for everyone.

"It's such a wonderful place!" exclaimed Vicky as Bob was taking a photo of her stood next to a display of orchids at an orchid farm they had stopped at for a while. "We shall have to come back, perhaps next year on our way to Australia."

Bob lowered his camera. "Who said we're going to Aussie?"

Vicky straightened her skirt. "I did – just now. We can go and see Ida. She'll love it."

Bob frowned. "But we haven't seen her for nearly thirty years."

"Then it's about time we did – after all, none of us are getting any younger."

Bob shook his head. There would never be any changing her, but he liked it that way. You never knew what she was going to come out with next. Besides, perhaps he could book the tickets to coincide with some sport fixtures – the rugby maybe? An idea began to grow. "Say cheese," he smiled and he clicked the camera.

Changi Airport was, as always, frantic in the evening. As such, not much time was given to the saying of farewells – though, in Noreen's case, it was more of a braying. She hated goodbyes, and, since it had been such a long time since the last time she had seen Jean, it made the parting that bit more difficult to endure. However, promises were made for them to get together again, and not to leave it so long.

Stuart and Barbara, much to their own surprise more than anything, gave up the opportunity to relax in the business-class lounge before boarding their flight, choosing to snoop around the array of duty-free shops together with Bob and Vicky.

Stuart and Vicky were enjoying a squabble with each other, and Bob had veered away to look at some watches, Barbara scuttling behind in his wake.

"Look, a Singapore batik-pattern umbrella. You would look quite the dandy parading along the high street in Boscombe with that held aloft."

Vicky savoured the comment, twirling the umbrella in a mocking fashion.

Stuart wasn't about to be outdone. "Tinkie la Trash would never allow it. Oh, it would look rather fetching, wouldn't it? but I fancy it's more of a Poole Harbour type of thing. We've just bought a stunning place – lovely views, established garden and all that jazz. You'll have to pop in for tea one afternoon if your senior citizen discount bus coupons will carry you that far. Come along, Vicks, let's go and see if the cosmetics here are any good. They might even have some anti-wrinkle cream new on the market. It might be a bit late, but you never know, and at these prices you'd be a fool not to take advantage!"

Vicky gurgled back at him, "Cheeky bitch! C'mon on, then – they might even have some haemorrhoid cream on special offer for you!" and with that the pair of them shrieked with laughter and disappeared into the crowds.

At Hector's request, they had all said goodbye to one another after the passport control. He then escorted his new wife to the First Class lounge, where they sat enjoying a drink before boarding their flight to Cape Town. At any given chance, he thrilled himself by saying, "My wife would like . . . ," or, "Do you think my wife could . . ." It made Jean giggle and feel young again.

They boarded the aircraft and settled into their seats – 3A and C. The plane taxied and idled away in the queue for take-off.

Looking out of the window, Jean nudged Hector each time a plane hurtled down the runway past them, and they both said at the same time, "Goodbye, Noreen," or, "Cheers, Aussies!" Though it may well not have been, the plane they chose as the one heading for London thundered by, and they grew quiet. "See you soon," they whispered. Before the sense of melancholy could affect them, it was their turn, and the captain requested the crew to take their seats for the take-off.

The flight climbed into the sky, and the newly-weds held hands and sipped their champagne.

A spot of dinner, maybe a movie, then a nap, and soon they would be sampling wines and enjoying all that the beautiful Cape Province has to offer visitors.

Behind the first-class compartment, Miss Tan, a senior flight attendant, mixed a Martini cocktail. Placing the glass on a tray with some canapés to accompany it, she floated down the aisle to the last row of the Raffles-class cabin. Leaning across to the passenger in the window seat, who was, like so many of the businessmen on her flights, preoccupied with some paperwork, she offered the tray, saying, "A Martini cocktail, Mr Lee, just as you asked – dry, and with a twist."